To Eileen

Coleraine

A Time Remembered

Coleraine

A Time Remembered

William Connor

Ballintoy

First published in 2010 by
Ballintoy Book Publishers
www.ColeraineRemembered.com

Copyright © 2010 by William Connor

ISBN – 13: 978-0-9865820-0-4

Cover design: Ballintoy Book Publishers
Cover photograph: *Bann Bridge*
Printed and bound in Canada

For my three children: John Mark
Sarah Kathleen and William Ryan

Foreword

My earliest memories of Ireland fade with each passing year and yet sometimes, quite unexpectedly, the wonder and beauty of the Ireland I knew returns, stirring within me memories of an enchanted land. And with each encounter I experience a yearning to return, to find a secluded corner in the Anderson Park where I might quietly reflect on what it was like growing up in a town without violence, a town where people lived in relative peace and harmony with one another. While in the park, I will remember my father and our leisurely Sunday afternoon walks together. Perhaps too, I will recall a different walk beyond the town and that warm summer evening in the grass, flushed with the excitement of first love. And like every other visit, I will experience the bittersweet memory of family and friends who have passed on and who were, for a time, such an important part of my life.

On my last visit to Ireland, not so long ago, I sat quietly watching the Irish Sea through a broken layer of cloud. Beneath us the Isle of Man flashed past and a short time later the Irish coast came into view. It began to rain as the aircraft banked to follow the shoreline of Belfast Lough on its final approach into Belfast City Airport. When the flight touched down on the wet tarmac I knew I was home once more, home to spend a week with my wife and family in a rented cottage near the Giant's Causeway, not far from the place where my mother was born and where, as a youngster, I happily spent a good part of my summer holidays each year.

The holiday, which had been planned months earlier, would bring the family together to explore the ancient land of their father's birth. Our three children, when they were much younger, had previously been to Ireland to visit their grandparents and to meet many of their relatives. Now that they were older and had families of their own they were anxious to experience Ireland for themselves. Over the next several days our youngest son and his wife would arrive in Dublin from San Diego and journey by train to Coleraine. His sister and her husband and our three year old granddaughter would arrive from Ottawa and travel by train to Belfast to spend a few days with my brother in Bangor. Our eldest son now living in the Carolinas would unfortunately be unable to join us. They were expecting their second child within a matter of weeks or even days.

During the course of the week that followed we drove for miles, often in the rain, exploring ancient towns and villages and historical sites that held a special interest for them. Together they witnessed the spectacular beauty of Ireland, often visiting out of the way places they had only heard about from their father, returning to the cottage each evening with a renewed sense of wonder and curiosity. It was not the Ireland they had read about or seen on television years earlier. It was instead a land of peace and growing prosperity, a land with a renewed spirit of hope and optimism for the future.

Someone once told me Ireland is not so much a place as a way of life where the present is held hostage to the past. There is much in Ireland's troubled history to suggest that might be true.

During our visit we were aware of people who still harbour anger and resentment at the cost of peace, others who were disappointed in the peace process itself, believing it did not go far enough, and some, including people I had known as a boy, who sadly live with the scars of this bloody conflict.

When the children left to return home, I wondered again why it had happened. Like others of my generation I was aware of many of the reasons: the suppression of a catholic minority and the deeply rooted religious intolerance and mistrust among people of different expressions of faith; the savage determination of some to break Britain's hold on Northern Ireland, and the resolve on the part of others to preserve what they thought was rightfully theirs, with the same wanton disregard for the cost in human life. Perhaps Willie Thompson is right. "There is no sense to be made out of it."

And yet, as I stood with my wife by the cottage on the last morning of our stay, there was in the air an undeniable sense of peace and a deepening awareness that a people's journey had begun.

William Connor

Railway Road
Tuesday 12 June 1973

Chapter One

No one seemed to notice the blue Ford Cortina entering the town. There was nothing unusual about its appearance or for that matter, about the two men who sat in the front seat. It was just another car making its way into Coleraine on a peaceful Tuesday afternoon.

At Society Street the car slowed and moments later came to a sudden halt a short distance from a police barricade that blocked the road ahead. On the other side of the barricade, less than a hundred yards from where they had stopped, a police constable stood beside the open door of a Land-Rover.

"Oh Jasus, what do we do now? There's no way I can get around that," the driver said, looking anxiously at the barricade and at the policeman who had stepped away from the Land-Rover and appeared to be looking in the opposite direction. It was then that he saw the submachine gun slung over his shoulder.

"Quick, turn the car around."

The driver, the younger of the two men, hesitated. "But this is where we're supposed to park it. That's what they told us."

"Would you forget about what they told us. Just turn the car around," the other man shouted excitedly.

"That's what I'm trying to do."

"Now....in the name of God do it now before that policeman sees us and wants to know what the hell we're doing stopped in the middle of the street."

The car backed up quickly, braked hard and spun around, narrowly missing a small electric milk cart parked on the opposite side of the road.

"And where are we supposed to go now?"

"I'm damned if I know."

"We're running out of time."

"Don't you think I know that....you just drive the bloody car until I figure something out."

"You can drop me off near the bottom of the Lodge Road if you like. That way you can go on up to the house without driving back through the town," Mary said, reaching for the canvas shopping bag at her feet.

"If that suits you."

"It does, and besides it's easier for you to stop there."

"Aye, it's handy enough."

As the car neared the top of Railway Road, Thompson stopped to let a pedestrian and a man on a bicycle cross in front of him before turning the car around and heading back up the Lodge Road.

"There's an empty spot, just ahead of us. And it's on our side of the road too."

Thompson nodded. "I see it." He pulled the car to the side of the road and rolled to a stop opposite the police barracks.

Mary reached across the seat and kissed him lightly on the cheek. "Would you fancy a wee bit of minced pork for supper? I

16

could do it up in the oven, if you like. It would make a nice change."

"Aye I would enjoy that."

"Well, then, I'll drop into the Pork Shop on my way back." He got out of the car and walked around to the passenger side to open her door. She took his hand and stepped gracefully onto the pavement.

"Thanks love, I'll see you later on." He smiled and released her hand. She carries herself well for a woman her age, he thought. It still gave him pleasure just to look at her. She caught his eye and smiled back at him. "Go on now...."

Closing the door he started back towards the driver's side.

"Is there anything else you need while I'm here?" she asked.

"Only the dry cleaning, but that can wait."

"No, sure for all the time it takes I may as well walk to the laundry while I'm at it. I'm going that way anyway and besides it'll save you having to make another trip into the town."

He paused to look at his watch. "Well, whatever you think then. Why don't I meet you here say in an hour or so if that will give you enough time to do what you have to do?"

"Oh, plenty. I won't even need that long. Sure I have only three or four wee things to get, but if you don't mind I think I'd prefer to walk back at my leisure. It's a lovely warm afternoon and the walk will do me the world of good." She raised her hand and waved cheerfully then turned and set off down the street at a good pace, her shopping bag swaying at her side.

He stood by the car for a few moments watching her turn the corner and disappeared up Railway Road. It was then the thought occurred to him that maybe he should leave the car where it was and go after her. The walk wouldn't do him any harm either. "No, I'll go home; there's work that needs to be done in the garden and today's as good a day as any to do it." he said aloud, opening the door and climbing back into the car. As

17

he did so, he heard the town hall clock strike the hour. Out of habit, he looked at his watch and smiled. It was exactly three minutes after two. As usual, the town clock, the four-faced-liar as it was known by everyone who lived in the town, was running a few minutes slow. Some things never change, he thought, as he started the car and waited for an opening in the flow of traffic that was moving slowly up the Lodge Road.

♣

"Mary Thompson, is that you?"

"Och, hello Mrs. Henry. It's nice to see you back on your feet again after your illness. It's been awhile since I've seen you on the street. "

"Aye it has, sure enough, but thank God I'm feeling rightly now. Mind you, I took another wee turn last week that set me back a bit, but I have to say I'm feeling more like myself today. The doctor says that at my age it'll come and go and he doesn't think there's much a body can do about it. So there you are...a lot of good he did me. For all he knows, I'd be as well off asking that oull cat of ours. Aye, that's the God's truth and I told him as much, so I did."

Mary smiled. "Well, the weather helps too."

"It does right enough. I've often said there's nothing like a spell of good weather to make us feel more like ourselves. It gives us a wee lift, right enough. We should take the good of it when we get the chance, that's what I say. God knows, it'll be a long oull cold winter if last year is anything to go by."

"Aye, I don't doubt it. But then the weather's not what it used to be."

"No....no it's not right enough," she said, nodding her head in agreement. "Mary, I've been meaning to ask you for some time how Molly is. God help her, I often think of her. She took a hard knock...you all did."

"Oh, she does the best she can. For awhile she was in bits, but sure that was to be expected. Now she takes one day at a time and like the rest of us tries to cope as well as she can. It's not easy mind you, even now."

"Dear God don't I know it. When our wee fellow was drowned in the Bann, I wanted to jump in myself, God forgive me for saying it. But I had the rest of them to think about and that's the only thing that saved me. God love him, he would have been fifteen on his next birthday. Passed his eleven plus too and he was the only one that did. God love him....I often wonder what he would have made of himself if he'd been spared to us. Now we'll never know."

Mary put her hand to her mouth and gently shook her head. "No....that's the truth. It was a terrible thing Mrs. Henry. We often wondered how you managed to cope when it happened. And little did we know at the time what was in store for us as well. But then sure nobody does, and God knows, it's probably just as well, although I've often said it doesn't make it any easier when it happens. It's a dreadful thing for a parent to lose a child. People often think they understand, but they don't, and there's no way they can until they've gone through it themselves. And God forbid that's something I wouldn't wish on anyone. It was a terrible loss, Mrs Henry and my heart goes out to you."

"Oh dear knows it was....it still is, but I'm sorry for your trouble too, Mrs Thompson, dear knows I am."

"It is kind of you to say so."

"They say time heals, but I'm not sure that it does. I can still see his lovely wee face. Sometimes out of nowhere I'll remember something he said or the way he looked at me when he said it. And God forgive me, I still get angry when I think of how he was taken from us at such an early age and him with everything to live for. Aye, right enough Mrs Thompson, you manage as best you can. Sure that's all any of us can do, no matter who we are, that's what I always say. Some days are

19

better than others, but you soldier on, for what else can you do?"

"Aye, aye, indeed." She was about to say something else, but changed her mind. Somehow there didn't seem to be much point in dwelling on it any longer.

"Be sure an' tell that man o' yours I was asking for him."

"I'll do that," she said, trying hard to smile.

"Well, I'll say cheerio now, Mrs Thompson. I've a few more wee messages to run at this end of the town before I head back over the Bann. I'm so glad I ran into you and had the chance to have a wee talk. You'll remember me to Molly too, won't you?"

"Aye, I will....Cheerio, then, Mrs Henry."

"Cheerio, and take care of yourself."

"Yes, and you too."

The Ford Cortina circled back through the town and started up Union Street. A short distance beyond the Technical School the driver braked as the car approached the corner of Brook Street.

"What are you doing now?" the other man hollered, making no attempt to hide his anger.

"I'm turning the car."

"Damn it man, not here.... did you not hear what I said a minute ago? I told you to drive on up to Railway Road. Now take your foot off the brake and don't stop again until we find somewhere to park this bloody thing, and be quick about it before it's too late."

A short time later the car turned onto Railway Road and soon after, the driver hurriedly pulled the car into an empty space between two cars and parked in front of a paint shop. Both men got out, closed the door behind them, and quickly disappeared into the crowd of shoppers milling about the street.

A second small car, as unobtrusive as the first, entered the town from the other side of the river and made its way across the

20

Bann. This time there was no hesitation; the driver knew exactly where he was going. The car slowed as it approached the Boathouse and then, quickly and decisively turned into Stuart's Garage in Hanover Place. At that moment, an apprentice mechanic saw a man park the car by the petrol pumps inside, remove the ignition key and run rapidly out of the garage.

Four Years Earlier
Autumn 1969

Chapter Two

The rain started falling early in the morning, a soft, damp, persistent drizzle that only added to the dreariness of the day. By late afternoon the wind shifted, sighed and gathered itself up, pushing a line of dark menacing clouds inland from the sea. As it reached the ancient town nestled on both sides of the Bann the wind increased in strength and the river, slowed in its progress to the sea, trailed a white rage upon its surface. When darkness fell, it began to rain heavier.

As he neared the river, Willie Thompson was having serious second thoughts about the wisdom of heading out on a night like this. It wasn't the first time the thought had occurred to him as he made his trek through the deserted streets of the town. The same thing had crossed his mind just minutes earlier when he reached the Diamond and started down towards the river. But he soldiered on hoping the rain might let up before he was completely soaked. At the bottom of Bridge Street he hurriedly stepped into the darkened doorway of Burns and Maguire's wireless shop. In the window a black and white television set had been left on to catch the eye of shoppers who were on the street earlier in the afternoon. Sheltered from the rain or at least the worst of it, Thompson stood in the narrow doorway for a moment watching the flickering black and white picture in the window. Years ago, he recalled one of his mates from Long Commons telling him skipper Burns had a real television set in the shop window. It was the first television he had ever seen and he remembered thinking how disappointed he was when together they had walked half way across the town just to see it. The screen was small and the picture didn't seem all that good and at the time he left wondering what all the excitement was about. The man in the screen was talking to someone, but there was no sound; it was like watching an old silent picture and not a very good one at that. Now they were calling it the telly, and although the picture was greatly improved, he still preferred the wireless and was in no hurry to replace it with an expensive television set. Somehow listening to the radio was a more rewarding experience. You only had to listen to conjure up images of people and places that were uniquely your own. It was a personal encounter much like being in the company of an old and familiar friend. He pulled a clean linen handkerchief from his overcoat pocket and wiped the rain from his face and the back of his neck. Sniffing the damp night air, he blew his nose and put the handkerchief back in his pocket. Now a woman joined the man on the silent screen. Aye, sure he would wait awhile and by then maybe the new coloured sets would be more to his liking and perhaps more affordable.

He stood in the sheltered doorway for a few moments longer to catch his breath and consider his options. Earlier, when he first walked out of the house at the other end of the town, it looked as if the rain might ease, at least long enough for him to make his way across the Bann. But now it was raining heavier than ever and to make matters worse it showed no signs of letting up. He could always head back, of course, but he'd come this far and had little inclination to turn back now. At this stage in the game, he reckoned he was just as likely to get drenched no matter what he decided. It also occurred to him that if he continued on across the river he'd at least have something to show for his trouble. The headlamps of a small car appeared out of nowhere, passed in front of him and just as quickly disappeared over Bann Bridge. The car was a kind of omen. Well, maybe not, but in the absence of anything better, it would do. His mind was made up. Without further thought, he pulled the collar of his overcoat tightly about his neck, stepped out onto the street, and started over the bridge, quickening his pace as he went.

A short time later he reached the other side of the river and quickly turned the corner into Killoween. Sheets of rain lashed the dark wet pavement, leaving large puddles of water scattered along the narrow street. On one side of the road, street lamps shook nervously in the wind. A few had gone out altogether leaving stretches of the street in darkness. Thompson smiled and wondered if the electric lamp had burned itself out or been shattered by a boy with a homemade catapult and a handful of stones. As a youngster, he had smashed more than his share of street lamps. In time he became an accomplished marksman of sorts boasting he could extinguish a gas lamp at a hundred yards or drive a stone up the arse end of a mare with little or no discomfort to the horse. Even now he wasn't sure why he had found it necessary to mention the horse at all, but at the time his exaggerated claim didn't seem to bother him and after awhile he almost came to believe it himself. No one had actually seen him put a stone up a mare's arse, but they had seen him break the glass on a street lamp with a single stone and take a window out of an abandoned warehouse with one easy shot. His pals seemed happy enough to believe that if he could do one he could probably do the other. Luckily no one had pressed him for a demonstration and when he announced one day that he had given it up out of consideration for the horse, it struck them as a reasonable enough explanation. The truth was he had tried it only once and had both his ears cuffed for his trouble. The horse had bolted down the street, spilling a bag of coal from a flat cart onto the road. The coalman, his red eyes glaring from beneath a coal bag draped over his head and shoulders to protect him from the rain, grabbed him by the arm with one hand and boxed his ears with the other. He swore between his yellow teeth that if he ever caught him doing such a stupid thing again he would shove a piece of black coal up his arse and a bloody big piece at that. He could smell the drink on his breath and was so scared he almost peed in his trousers. It could have been worse for the coalman knew his father and mother and there would have been the devil to pay had they found out.

When one of the boys was nabbed by the police, they wisely abandoned their interest in street lamps and instead took to wandering down the Calf Lane, at the other end of the town, in search of new and more challenging targets. At the foot of the railway embankment, just beyond a row of brick and stucco houses, they found a perfect place to hide in the long grass while they waited for trains that puffed and rattled their way to the seaside towns of Portstewart and Portrush. As the train passed directly above them they rose from their hiding place, took aim and quickly released their catapults. Some of the stones struck the side of the coach as the train gathered speed and disappeared down the track trailing a cloud of dark billowing smoke. Just before the end of summer and their return to school a guard on one of the trains reported them to the railway authorities. A police constable caught them red handed a few days later as they released their catapults on a passing train. A short time later a member of the constabulary arrived unannounced at the front door of the modest two storey house his father rented in Long Commons. It was the same big policeman who had written his name down in a book a month earlier for attempting to climb through the window of a vacant house in Bell House Lane.

Sometime later, he and his father appeared in the old courthouse at the foot of Captain Street. The magistrate turned out to be a stern, but kindly old man who admonished him to mend his ways before he found himself in far more serious trouble. As instructed, he told the court he had learned his lesson and that he was deeply sorry for all the trouble he had caused. The old magistrate took him at his word and placed him on probation, much to the relief of his anxious parents. His father, he remembered, had lost half a day's pay. Funny thing, he thought, shaking his head in silent remembrance of what his father had done so long ago. I had forgotten all about that. Half a day's pay was a lot of money.

A few years later, he was back in the same courtroom for borrowing an Austin Seven that belonged to the Church of Ireland curate. He had lifted the car at the bottom of Union Street and with some difficulty coached it onto the Portrush Road and set off for the coast at a good clip. As he approached the sharp turn at the Shell Hill bridge his foot reached for the brake, but instead of slowing down the car accelerated, and before he could correct his mistake the car struck the stone wall damaging a headlamp and the left front mudguard. To make matters worse he was so badly shaken that he lost control of the car. The Austin left the road and ploughed through a hedge coming to rest in a field on the wrong side of the road.

The next morning the police arrived at the front door, summons in hand, looking for a Willie Thompson who lived in Long Commons. As luck would have it he was still in his bed and would happily have remained there for the rest of the day. His father had already left for work leaving his poor mother to cope as best she could. She hadn't coped very well. "Well, you can't see him... his father will have to deal with it and he's left for his work. You'll have to come back," she told them, quickly closing the door before they had time to protest. He jumped to the window and watched them disappear down the street. They would be back, and what was even worse, he'd have to face the music a second time when his father came home from work. He pulled the blanket over his head just as his mother reached the top of the stairs.

A month later he appeared before the magistrate, only this time he wasn't so lucky. The police sergeant stood up and rattled on about one thing and another, pausing now and again to turn another page in the small black notebook he held in one of his large hands. He was no help at all particularly when he told the court young Thompson was well known to the constabulary and in recent months had been a constant source of trouble for the police in Coleraine. He remembered thinking at the time, that big fellow's got it in for me. Another man got up and told the magistrate what it would cost to fix the Austin Seven. He wasn't too helpful either.

The old magistrate sat without moving a muscle, for what seemed like a very long time. With his head down and his hands clasped together, he sat staring at the leather bound journal lying open on the bench in front of him. Earlier, Willie had watched him write something down on the page with a black and blue marble fountain pen. It looked expensive. He would like a pen like that someday and wondered if he could pinch one from Miss Wood's bookshop on Church Street without getting caught. The magistrate picked up the fountain pen and again started to scribble something on the page. When he had finished, he carefully screwed the top back on and set it down on the bench. He rubbed his hand along his chin and looked directly at the young man standing before him as if trying to size him up.

"What's he doing now? I wish to God he'd take his eyes off me."

"What's that you said?"

"Nothing, I was just muttering to myself."

The old man paused before he spoke again. "Haven't I seen you before?"

He decided to say nothing in case the old boy was trying to trick him. If he gave the wrong answer it would only make matters worse. And besides, he knew friggin well that he had, but he wasn't about to tell him, on the off chance he'd forgotten, although that didn't seem too likely. He looked like a crafty old bugger, right enough.

"I asked you a question."

"Aye, you did," he whispered.

"Speak up boy, I can hardly hear you."

The old bugger's not going to let up, he thought, as he tried to figure out his next move. He was quickly running out of options and he doubted there was much he could do to improve his situation.

"Well, boy?"

"Aye...well."

"Well, what?"

"Aye you have your worship."

"I thought so."

He lowered his eyes and stared nervously at his feet. His father had bought him a new pair of shoes so that he would look more presentable. How he looked was important his father had told him. He'd also told him to stand straight, and to put his shoulders back, and to look at the magistrate when he spoke to him. In his present circumstance it was a hard thing to do, but he knew his father was right for he had told him these things only out of concern for his welfare. He had done the best he could to follow his father's advice, but his anxiety made it difficult to look the old man in the face when he spoke. He thought too, that if he did his eyes might somehow betray him. It was less threatening just to lower his head and gaze at his feet. They were a nice pair of shoes, all shiny and new, and as he stood gazing at his feet, it dawned on him that he might not be able to wear them again for some time. It was then that he realized just how much trouble he was in. He recalled too, that the day before, his mother had wiped down his only suit with a damp cloth and ironed the jacket and trousers. His father thought maybe he should have a new one, but money was scarce and his mother said they would have to make do. And right enough, when she was through with it, it looked alright.

"Is there anything you want to say?"

He shook his head.

"You're quite sure?"

He could almost feel the glare of the old man's eyes on him. I suppose now is as good a time as any, he thought, to apologize, to the court, for what he had done. It had worked before, and maybe with a bit of luck it might work again, he told himself, not altogether convincingly.

"Aye, well….maybe only to say that I'm really sorry."

"You're what?"

"I'm sorry for all the trouble I have caused. I honestly don't know what else to say, your honour. It was a stupid thing to do, and that's the God's truth."

"You're sorry....is that what you're telling me?"

"Aye... I am your worship."

"You're sorry, is that it!"

Remembering again what his father had said, he gathered up what he could of his courage and lifting his head as high as he dared he looked directly at the magistrate. "Aye, that's what I said, sir... I'm deeply sorry for all the trouble I've caused everybody."

"Well....well."

"I am...." he heard himself whisper.

"You told me that once before."

He stared at his feet again in an effort to regain his composure.

"I did...."

"And I took you at your word, didn't I?"

"Yes, you did your worship." Holy mackerel, the old boy's got a better memory than I thought. Who would believe an old man that age would remember anything, let alone what I said the last time he saw me.

"Well, then, maybe you can tell us what possessed you to take the car in the first place."

"I don't know..."

"You don't know!"

"I don't...I don't know what got into me."

"You don't know what came over you, is that what you're telling us?"

He nodded. God I wish he would stop repeating everything I say.

"So that's it, you acted on impulse?"

"I believe I did your honour."

The magistrate hesitated. "Well tell me, do you have any appreciation at all of the amount of damage you caused to the Reverend Boyd's motorcar?"

"Aye...sure, didn't I hear your man over there?" he said, pointing to the small man who had provided the estimate on how much it would cost to fix the car and who now sat a short distance away looking very pleased with himself.

The Magistrate ignored him. "You have caused a great deal of damage, to say nothing of the harm you might have inflicted on innocent people. You're a very fortunate young man that no one was injured as a result of your wilful and reckless behaviour."

"Aye, sure enough. Mind you, it was an old wreck of a car to begin with, your worship, and how was I supposed to know it belonged to the Church of Ireland? And I'll tell you another thing, that wee curate should have locked that car. One of these days he's going to lose something out of it."

There was a brief outburst of laughter from the back of the courtroom follow by an abrupt silence.

"That's enough, that's enough of that. And look at me when I speak to you. You're old enough to know better," the magistrate said, impatiently, raising his voice and pointing an accusing finger directly at him.

Jesus, the old eyes are on me again.

33

"And you're from a decent family."

He lowered his head and closed his eyes. Now he wanted to hide, to run away from the place. He had not meant to say what he had just said, it just came out of him and he knew it would only make matters worse. God knows he had been told often enough to watch what he said.

"Well, boy."

"Aye..." he whispered.

"Speak up. I can't hear you."

He could feel his heart pounding. "Yes, I come from a good family.... I know that." He thought of his dad and struggled to hold back the tears.

The magistrate looked over to where his parents were sitting in silence and slowly shook his head. "Your parents deserve better, don't you think son," he said, kindly.

He nodded and tried to answer, but the words would not come. Again, he fought to hold back the tears that were welling up inside him.

There was another long and awkward silence and for a few moments the old man just sat there staring beyond the witness box, his hand pressed against his mouth. It was almost as if he was struggling with himself over the determination he had already made. Clearing his throat, he closed the leather bound journal and carefully set his glasses down on the bench beside it. He looked directly at the young man standing in front of him and then turned to address his parents. "I'm sorry, but this time I have little choice, you know, but to send him to Derry... I hope it will do him some good," he said earnestly.

The old man had said something else, but he had long forgotten what it was. He saw the sergeant rise and walk towards him. He remembered seeing his father reach out and put his arm around his mother as she tried to hide her tears with the back of her open hand. A few moments later a constable led him out through the side door of the court house to a waiting police van.

Years later, his mother told him how pale and frightened he looked as he turned back to wave at them standing in the street. Even now, he could still see them standing huddled together in the rain. He remembered too, the pain in his father's eyes. The door closed behind him shutting out the street.

He could no longer see his mother's face. He couldn't see anything, only the drab grey interior of the cold damp van and the large policeman who sat opposite him with a package of cigarettes in his hand. "Here lad, you look as if you could use one." He put the cigarette to his mouth as the van lurched forward. His head fell back against the inside of the van and he closed his eyes and wept. Never again would he allow himself to be so foolish. For the first time in his young life he was really afraid.

A year after he returned home his father died, and for a time he went to work in the gas works for a few shillings a week. His mother, he remembered, had told him tearfully that his father had a hard life and his heart just gave out.

The wind shifted as he lowered his head and shoulders into the driving rain. His thoughts turned to a happier time. To the carefree days he had spent in the company of friends with no more sense than himself. Together they had robbed orchards on the Lodge Road, almost within sight of the police barracks, filling their pockets with apples that were always too sour to eat. But that didn't seem to matter, for more often than not, the apples were thrown back over the wall or left to rot on the side of the road. The prize was the excitement and sometimes the fear they felt as they climbed over the wall to pinch a handful of apples without being caught by the police or the people who lived in the big houses at the top of the Lodge Road. One of the boys was always left on the wall to keep dick and to warn them if someone was coming. If someone approached before they could scramble back over the wall, they crouched low in the orchard without making a sound until the coast was again clear.

That was the really scary part.

He recalled too, climbing the wall of the old chapel at the head of Long Commons, to throw stones and shout insults at smartly dressed boys and girls his own age, who carried their bibles to church on Sunday morning. Sometimes, the bigger girls in the group shouted back defiantly and stuck their tongues out at their tormentors as they ran off skipping and jumping down the street.

Sticks and stones may break my bones,
But names will never hurt me.
When I'm dead and in my grave,
You'll suffer for what you called me.

And on Saturday evenings, when they had nothing better to do, they gathered in the centre of the town to heckle the Salvation Army at their open air meeting. From a safe distance, they taunted the small group of Salvationists standing reverently in a circle bearing witness to the saving power of the blood of the Lamb.

The Salvation Army free from sin,
Went to heaven in a corned beef tin;
The tin toppled over and they all fell out,
And they all went to heaven the other way about.

Seldom did they remain more than a few minutes, just long enough to disrupt the meeting, and then for fear of being caught, they turned and ran as fast as their legs would carry them, until they were finally out of breath. Afterwards, they hid in the Anderson Park until they could no longer hear the sound of the Army's big drum. He remembered too, that sometimes when he was alone, he stood at a distance quietly listening to the brass band and the words of testimony from men who said they had been saved from all sorts of terrible things.

But summer was always more fun, for the days were long and warm and they spent their time looking for eels or bathing naked in the river until the last rays of sunlight disappeared over the Mount. When it rained, and in Ireland it often did, they stayed indoors and played pitch and toss, or played devil's cards and drank brown vinegar out of cheap plastic egg cups, just like the cowboys they had seen at the cinema.

Sometimes, he walked across the street and played doctor with the two Kennedy girls when their mother went off to collect the allowance. The twins were a few years older and very experienced in all sorts of things. They had a wonderful knowledge of the human anatomy and you could always count on a thorough examination from the pair of them. And they were not a bit shy either. But the best part, he remembered, was when it was your turn to conduct the examination. They were both lovely girls and didn't mind at all if you unbuttoned their blouse in the interests of medical science. They were also a great help in showing you the nicest places to put your hand. It was a lovely way to spend an hour and educational as well, sort of like looking for things that were never lost. That's what they used to say. "Do you want to find something that isn't lost?" Strange, the things you remember, he thought. One of the twins had died, and the other had gone with her mother to find a better life, somewhere in England. He hoped they had found it.

It was raining heavier now as he reached the top of the hill and started down the other side. He felt damp and uncomfortable. Large drops of water trickled down the side of his face and ran down the back of his neck. Yet in spite of his discomfort, he stoically regarded the rain as a constancy in his life that bound the past and the present together. It endured from one generation to another, and on each generation it cast its spell and changing moods on the land and its people.

Music floated across the river, and from the brow of the hill he could see the dark shadow of Bann Bridge, and the lights of the

Boathouse dancing on the water below. Someone was singing, for the wind carried the words of The Kerry Dance.

O' the days of the Kerry dancing,
O' the ring of the piper's tune!
O' for one of those hours of gladness,
Gone, alas! like our youth too soon....

He thought again of the past, of the market, where men carried bibles in their tattered coat pockets and swore to God that the cattle and sheep they were selling were among the best in all of Ireland. They would arrive early in the morning, driving their cattle through the narrow streets of Coleraine, shouting and cursing all the way to New Market Street. They were coarse men, but not beyond kindness. It was the smell of the market that he remembered most of all: the heavy odour of fresh horse piss and cow shit mingled with straw, and the smell of the men who bartered and cursed and prodded cattle with sticks, until they shat from fright, and slipped and fell in their own droppings. He remembered too, the smell of the little drab pubs that lined the one side of New Market Street where men and women drank and cursed youngsters who poked their heads in through the door and asked for a penny.

It was here, not long after he returned from Derry, he met Maggie McGuire who first invited him into her bed. Maggie was in her late twenties or so she had told him, but he had always thought she was much older than she let on. And once, at the very beginning, when she had offered him something to drink he had vomited on the street outside her house and she had watched him from the window. He was not the only one to jump into Maggie's bed, but at the time that didn't seem to matter, one way or the other. It was just something he never thought much about. Her love making was spontaneous and uninhibited. Maggie was not one to waste a lot of time on foreplay and it seldom amounted to anything more than pulling her knickers down and spreading herself on the bed.

He often visited the house in Long Commons, sometimes two or three times a month, and on each occasion she opened her door and invited him in. Only if there was someone else in the house did she hold the door and discreetly tell him to call another time. And sometimes, quite unexpectedly, she received him with a warmth and tenderness that touched him more deeply than he cared to admit.

He recalled too his last visit to Maggie's house a few months before she died. She didn't seem to be herself somehow, for after it was over she remained on the bed gazing into the open hearth.

"I had a dream last night," she said softly.

She waited for him to say something, but he said nothing.

"And when I woke up, I wasn't sure where I was."

"Och.... sure it happens sometimes."

It wasn't so much what she said for there was nothing odd about having a dream; but it was the way she said it that caught him off guard. Maggie was never a great one for engaging in conversation afterwards. Most of the time he got dressed and left the way he came in with no more than a casual exchange on the way out the door. He hadn't noticed when she first spoke, but now he could see tears in her eyes and it made him feel uncomfortable. He was not used to this kind of thing and he reproached himself for not getting out of the house sooner.

"Willie..."

Still unsure of himself, he hesitated, reluctant to say anything for fear he might say the wrong thing.

"Did you hear what I just said?" She paused to catch her breath, then got up and sat on the edge of the small bed.

"Aye, I did...."

There was something else about her he hadn't noticed, a sadness in her voice that left him wondering if he had stumbled into a private place where he did not belong, a place where he would rather not be.

"What is it Maggie.... what's bothering you?"

"Oh, nothing..." She sighed deeply, and holding herself in her arms she pulled her knees tightly against her stomach and began to rock gently on the bed. "Sure it's only a dream.... a silly old dream."

"Maggie, don't cry."

"I'm sorry....I just don't know what's come over me."

"There now...."

"Ooh, Willie!"

He lit a cigarette and handed it to her.

"Thanks." She wiped her eyes with her hand, and after a few moments handed the cigarette back.

"Feel better?"

"Maybe a wee bit."

"Do you want me to stay?"

"If you like, perhaps just for a minute or two."

"Are you going to be alright?"

Maggie nodded, "I think so...."

"Would it help if you talked about it?"

"It might."

"Well, then...."

"Oh, it was only a dream.... I don't remember how I got there, but I was in a great house in County Sligo and I wore a green velvet dress that reached all the way to the floor. My hair was soft and fine and I wore a necklace that glittered in the sun. There were servants too, and when they spoke to me they called me Miss Margaret. And outside the great house there was a garden, and a stream, and a bed of white roses." She lifted her head and wiped her tears with the corner of the bed sheet.

"Mother of God, a bed of white roses," she cried, and in her nakedness she turned from him and wept.

He watched her for a moment in silence and then, in the darkness, reached out awkwardly and took her hand.

40

"There...there, now."

"Oh God, Willie, don't you see?"

"Let it go."

"No! Don't you see? It's the roses.... the white roses."

But he had not seen, at least not at the time. Now perhaps he understood and he wondered what would have become of her had she lived to grow old. He would never know of course, and perhaps it was just as well, for Maggie it seemed belonged to no one, not even to herself.

There had been other women in his young life, but they were mostly girls his own age, naive and inexperienced who were more of a tease than anything else. Some were more fun than others, and some he hardly remembered their names. But there was one he remembered fondly, who always seemed to know what she wanted and pleasured herself on the grass behind the high wall of the Irish Society School or against the fence in the lane behind her house on Mount Street.

From the river below he heard the muted sounds of the dance band striking up the last verse of The Kerry Dance. He could no longer hear the words, but it didn't matter for he knew them by heart and in his head he sang the last verse of the song.

Time goes on and the happy years are dead,
And one by one the merry hearts are fled;
Silent now is the wild and lonely glen,
Where the bright glad laugh will echo ne'er again,
Only dreaming of days gone by in my heart I hear

Loving voices of old companions,
Stealing out of the past once more
And the sound of the dear old music,
Soft and sweet as in days of yore....

A moment later he crossed the street, pushed open the door,

and walked into Doherty's pub.

Chapter Three

It was raining heavily along the Antrim coast as the army lorry slowed and came to a halt on the outskirts of Ballintoy. On this stretch of the road, fog rolling in from the sea made driving difficult for the tall ruggedly built man who sat bent over the steering wheel, his eyes fixed on the road ahead. Directly in front of the lorry, a bank of fog hung over the road reducing visibility to a few yards. He looked at his wrist watch, then at the smaller man who sat in silence huddled against the opposite door pulling on a cigarette. The other man hadn't opened his mouth since leaving Bushmills. They were running late and the big man silently reproached himself for not starting out earlier on account of the weather. For whatever reason, it had not dawned on him that the weather would be this bad along the coast. There was no fog on the road when they left Coleraine, only rain and occasional patches of mist that gave him no cause for concern. It was only after they left Bushmills and neared the coast that the weather began to deteriorate rapidly. Still, heavy fog was common enough on the coast road, especially at this time of the year and its sudden appearance should have come as no surprise to him. He had lived long enough in Ireland to know how unpredictable the weather can be in winter. To make matters worse, they had run into a road block at the war memorial in Bushmills. He hadn't anticipated that either and it bothered him that the possibility hadn't occurred to him. It bloody well should have, he acknowledged, as he shifted his weight on the seat and stared into the wall of fog just beyond the headlights. As things turned out they had been lucky, damned lucky if the truth be told. The British Army uniforms had done the trick. And after what amounted to nothing more than a routine exchange and a few brief words about the weather, they were on their way again. Brendan Meagher was grateful too for the time he had spent in England. His cultivated English accent left something to be desired, but it had saved the day just the same. The young police constables appeared none the wiser. Two British soldiers in an army lorry were hardly anything to be concerned about. Besides, it was a miserable night and they had no intention of standing in the middle of the road a minute longer than was absolutely necessary. They waved them on and climbed back into the Land-Rover, thankful to be out of the rain. It was just as well for Meagher would have shot them without a moment's hesitation had they got in his way.

He eased the clutch out and the lorry started forward, hugging the grass dyke on the side of the road. The wipers snapped back and forth loudly as he peered through the windshield searching the road ahead for the fork off the main road that would take them to the small deserted harbour.

"Would you look at that?"

The small man sniffed the damp air and leaned forward on his seat, not quite sure what it was he was supposed to be looking at.

"Look at what?"

"Fog....the bloody fog, what else?

"Jasus," the small man said, indifferently, wiping his nose on his coat sleeve, "I can see that well enough, I'm not blind."

"Well, keep your eyes on your side of the road, then, I can't see a damned thing out there from where I sit."

"Aye, well, that makes two of us."

The lorry came to an abrupt stop as the road ahead suddenly disappeared in a solid wall of fog and rain. "Christ.... at this rate it'll take us all bloody night," Meagher said, banging his fist on the steering wheel. For the next several minutes both men stared into the grey darkness beyond the windshield as they waited for the patch of heavy fog to drift across the road. Meagher glanced quickly at his watch and shook his head in disbelief. It had taken them more than twenty minutes to cover a few short miles. Now he could only hope that the weather would delay the other fellows as well. It was small comfort, but it was better than nothing. He sat for a moment trying to sort out just exactly where on the road they might be. They had to be close, but just how close was anybody's guess. The trouble was that in this fog it would be easy enough to miss the secondary road altogether. He dismissed the thought as quickly as it had arisen. There was too much at stake to contemplate the possibility of failure. They had to arrive at the rendezvous on time or as close to it as possible.

"Damn this weather," he shouted angrily, as he struggled to spread the Ordnance Survey map of the North Antrim coast over the steering wheel.

The other man nodded indifferently. The weather was the least of his worries; what the hell did the big man beside him expect? Sure hadn't it rained all week and for the last couple of days fog had been reported off and on along the Antrim and Derry coast. Stupid bugger, he thought, as he picked a small piece of tobacco from the tip of his tongue, before sticking the cigarette back in his mouth. Aye, the big man was upset, he could see that plain enough. Too bloody bad....

"Hand me the torch."

"I haven't got it."

"You're useless."

"Sure, didn't you put it away yourself."

"Och, never mind."

"Suit yourself." And while you're at it, you can stick it up your arse if you can find it in this fog, he thought, quickly turning his head towards the window so that Meagher wouldn't see the broad smile spreading across his face.

Meagher reached down under the seat groping for the flashlight with his hand, swearing aloud as he did so. A few seconds later he retrieved it from the floor under the seat.

The other man sniggered.

"What the hell's so funny?"

"Nothin'...."

"It's no laughing matter."

"Well, I didn't say it was."

With his finger Meagher tapped lightly on the spot marked Ballintoy, then slowly moved it back along the road they were on. "There... right there." He tapped his finger again, this time on the place where a small secondary road joined the main road. The junction he was looking for was no more than half a mile from the village. His index finger moved slowly backwards along the main road as far as Lisnagunogue. With the flashlight he checked the odometer reading he'd taken earlier, then the distance marked on the map. It appeared to be the same. "There, would you look there!" he said, pointing to the map again.

"Aye, well, where the hell is it, then?"

"It's bloody well there, that's where it is,"

The small man from County Wicklow glanced across at the map, then at the blanket of fog beyond the headlights. He had worked with Meagher before and knew better than to say too much for fear the big man sitting in the driver's seat beside him would take it the wrong way. He was a moody bastard at the best of times. But whatever else he thought of Meagher, and most of it was best left unsaid, he knew he was in the company of a man who would do whatever was asked of him and sometimes more, without so much as blinking an eyelid.

The Irish Republican Army knew they could count on Meagher. Two years earlier his wife had been accidentally shot and killed by a police patrol at the border crossing south of Newry. A month later he calmly walked into a pub on the outskirts of Belfast and ordered a large whiskey. Minutes later he shot a young RUC constable through the head, and then simply vanished.

Scotland Yard's Special Branch code named him Chimaera after the mythical Greek monster that was part goat, and part snake, a cunning, ruthless terrorist who killed on demand. He was wanted in England for the murder of a police constable near the Old Bailey and for other acts of suspected terrorism on the British mainland. He moved quickly from place to place to avoid detection and for the past twelve months security forces in Britain had no idea of his whereabouts.

The fog appeared to lift slightly as Meagher folded the Ordnance Survey Map and placed it under his seat. He hurriedly rolled down the window and leaning forward stuck his head through the open window searching the road ahead as the lorry started to edge its way forward again. A few yards ahead, he spotted the secondary road leading to the harbour.

"There!"

"Where?"

"There for Christ sake, look over there," Meagher shouted, pointing through the fog.

The Wicklow man eased himself forward searching the road immediately in front of them.

"Now do you see it?"

"No... not yet."

"Are you that blind? Look, it's right there....on your side of the road."

The lorry stopped again, only this time with a sudden jerk that

47

drove the smaller man against the windscreen. His head struck the glass with a dull thud. "Goddam it...."

"I bet that bloody well hurt. Maybe you'll see better now," Meagher said, without the slightest hint of remorse.

"Och, it's nothing....sure I'm alright," he grunted, regaining his composure as best he could to avoid giving the big man beside him further cause to gloat at his expense. But already he could feel a bump beginning to rise on the side of his forehead. Jasus, I bet that hurt, what kind of a thing is that to say? Bloody right it hurts. Your head would hurt too after a wallop like that, he thought, biting his lip against the pain.

"Right, then... then let's get on with it. I'm going to need your help. The road's narrow and it drops off steeply just above the harbour, so whatever you do keep your eyes glued to the road or it'll be the end of both of us if we miss the turn and go over the edge."

"I take it you've been in here before?" The small man asked nervously.

"I have, but not on a night like this. It's a bad spot at the best of times, but in this kind of weather a man needs to have all his wits about him and a bit of luck thrown in as well, to drive a lorry down this road."

Meagher's answer did little to reassure him. "Jasus, I hope you know what you're doing, then. I didn't come all this way to drive over a cliff in the middle of nowhere."

Ignoring him, Meagher released the clutch and the lorry turned slowly off the main road into the narrow road that led down into Ballintoy harbour. A few minutes later they negotiated a sharp right turn at the gates of a small white church just visible in the headlights, then another sharp turn, this time to the left, before reaching the narrowest part of the road that dropped steeply to the harbour.

"Well, here goes." Meagher's voice was tense. "Mind what I said now. Keep your eyes on your side of the road. I think the

48

drainage ditch is on that side. If we catch a wheel we'll never get her out, and if we miss the turn we won't have to worry about the lorry or anything else for that matter."

"We'll know soon enough," the Wicklow man stammered, putting on a brave face, as the lorry moved slowly forward and began the steep treacherous descent down the narrow winding road.

Relieved to have reached the harbour without incident, Meagher pulled into a small clearing cradled against the cliff face. Cautiously he turned the lorry around so that it was facing back up the road and parked beside an abandoned fisherman's hut. The placed was deserted. He switched off the engine and waited. From where they sat overlooking the harbour, both men would be able to spot what they were looking for. Meagher hadn't said anything to the other man, but he knew that finding the small sheltered bay on a night like this would be a risky business. It would take a hell of a lot of skill and just as much luck, more luck than he had needed to get the lorry to the bottom of the road. But it wasn't impossible either, he reckoned, reaching for a cigarette and handing the Woodbines to the man seated beside him, who was now staring intently at the ghostly shadow of the breakwater a few hundred feet in front of them. He couldn't be certain, but the fog didn't appear to be quite as thick here as it was on the road.

Both men sat in silence listening to the roar of the sea and the rain beating against the windshield. The wall of fog reached almost to the surface of the water. Meagher struck a match and looked anxiously at his watch. The boat was late. Out of the corner of his eye he watched the Wicklow man puffing nervously on the cigarette he had given him, but what he was unaware of was the sense of uneasiness haunting the other man since crossing the border into the North earlier in the week. He blew out the match and returned his gaze to the darkness outside. If something went wrong there was only one narrow road leading back onto the main road. They were vulnerable and Meagher knew it and the longer they waited, the more they put themselves at risk. It was not a good place to be if they were discovered. The man beside him was no fool and he would know that too.

"Let's hope they're not too bloody late," Meagher said, glancing again at the wall of fog lying over the water.

"You can say that again...."

"Aye, but then again....maybe they've come and gone."

"Ooh, Jasus, don't say that."

"Don't be too sure, them boys aren't in the habit of hanging around too long, and who would blame them?"

The small man was acutely aware of their predicament and he didn't needed Meagher reminding him. He had enough on his plate to deal with. He wasn't sure what it was that was causing him so much anxiety, but whatever it was, he'd been unable to shake it and the drink hadn't helped. It wasn't the first time he'd been apprehensive, but somehow this was different, and it was beginning to play on his mind. The waiting didn't help either and the sooner they dragged their sorry arses out of here and back onto the main road the better it would be for both of them. Things in the six counties had taken a bad turn in recent months, and he wasn't sure it was all for the better. Then again, maybe he was beginning to take this whole sordid business too seriously. Perhaps it was time to give it up and return to his home in the Wicklow Mountains. But that, he knew from the experience of others, was easier said than done. Once in, it was difficult to get out. Born to a poor family in Tullamore he'd spent most of his youth wandering the Irish countryside looking for steady work until he was recruited by the Irish Republican Army. He was sent abroad for a time to learn his trade and since then he'd known nothing else. The last few years seemed like a lifetime and he was beginning to feel old beyond his years. "Maybe I'm not cut out for this business after all," he muttered, as he threw the cigarette butt to the floor and stamped it out with his foot.

Meagher heard it first. "Listen....there's our man."

"Where?"

"There....over there," Meagher shouted impatiently.

There was no mistaking the deep rumbling sound of powerful marine diesels. Within minutes, the engines stopped and both men heard the anchor drop into the sea a few hundred feet from where they sat. The large fishing boat was invisible in the fog, but it was out there, and it now lay at anchor in deep water riding a moderate swell just outside the entrance to the harbour.

The lorry's headlamps flashed quickly on and off. The Wicklow man raised his arm and pointed in the direction of the breakwater as three short beams of light penetrated the fog. Both men climbed down from the lorry and walked across a small stretch of sand and limestone to the water's edge. Meagher reached inside the heavy topcoat and pulled a service revolver from its holster; he removed the safety and placed the weapon in the large outside pocket on the right-hand side of his coat. He felt better now knowing that things had gone more or less as planned in spite of the inclement weather. But Meagher was not about to take anything for granted; it was not that he expected trouble, only that he had learned from bitter experience to be prepared to deal with the unexpected.

There was a brief commotion on deck as a rowboat was lowered into the water and carefully loaded with three wooden crates. Two crew members wearing yellow oilskins and sou'westers stepped down into the small wooden boat that was rising and falling on the swell. The older of the two picked up the oars and started for the mouth of the harbour. Meagher finished his cigarette and waited with the other man for the boat to reach the harbour.

Through the fog the shape of the boat came into view as it rounded the breakwater and entered the sheltered waters of the harbour. A dark figure was standing in the bow directing a low beam of light onto the water just ahead of the boat. The oarsman

51

made directly for the two shadowy figures standing a few feet from the shoreline. The bottom of the boat struck the sand and the two seamen jumped into the shallow water and hauled the boat onto the slip.

"You're just in time," Meagher shouted.

One of the men grunted something, breathing deeply from the strain of pulling the bow of the heavily loaded boat out of the water.

"I was beginning to wonder if you had given up."

"Aye, well..." The man paused to catch his breath. "I damned near did. We almost ran aground off Sheep Island. Had to bring her around the other side. It's a bitch of a night out there. Worst goddamned night I've put to sea in for a long time."

"It's a bloody good thing the skipper knows this coast as well as he does," the second man shouted.

Meagher nodded. "Well, it's a nice piece of work just the same. I'll grant you that."

"Aye, by God, it is that, but I won't do it again. Not for all the bleeding money in China. And you can tell that to your friends in the Irish Free State."

Meagher didn't bother to reply. Instead, he turned and walked quickly back to the lorry.

Both seamen set to work unloading the wooden crates and carrying them up the slip to the back of the waiting lorry. Meagher held the flashlight in his left hand while the Wicklow man opened each crate in turn and checked its contents. The larger of the three crates contained American AR-18 assault rifles. The remaining boxes were packed with high explosives, timing devices, and 45mm ammunition.

"Aye, it's all there."

"It bloody well better be all there."

"Oh, it's there."

Meagher nodded. "Right, then, let's get them loaded... I want to get the hell out of here, and quickly."

After the crates were secured in the back of the lorry, Meagher turned to the older of the two men and handed him a large sealed envelope. The man took the envelope, but said nothing. He knew all too well, that when you dealt with this crowd you kept your mouth shut and made sure others did the same. Whatever was happening tonight, on this god forsaken Irish coast, was no concern of his. He had his money and he was now anxious to get his boat out into the relative safety of the open sea. With any luck they would be back in Scotland before dawn and the British Navy would be none the wiser.

They watched the two men climb into the boat and disappear again into the bank of fog beyond the harbour. The Wicklow man climbed into the back as Meagher hurriedly started the lorry and slipped the gearbox into low gear. Coaching the heavily loaded lorry back up the steep winding narrow road, he knew, would be difficult and dangerous. This time the lorry had to keep moving if they were to reach the top of the road safely. A short time later, much to his relief, he turned onto the main road and started down into the village of Ballintoy.

In the back of the lorry, the Wicklow man had his own work cut out. He was an explosives' expert and regarded as one of the best in the business. Only occasionally did he feel any guilt at all about his work. It had to be that way; otherwise he couldn't do what he had to do and live with himself. He often wondered if bomber pilots had felt the same way when they dropped their bomb loads on cities throughout Germany. Like them, he was told it was something that had to be done; it was no longer a matter of choice. There was no other way to force Britain to abandon her interest in Northern Ireland. That's what they said and in the beginning he believed it. Now he was not so sure.

Turning on the small portable dome light he had rigged earlier in the evening before leaving Coleraine, he reached into the wooden crate closest to him and carefully removed two bundles of high explosives. Wrapping them tightly together with insulating tape he began the delicate job of wiring the detonator and the timing device. From his pocket he retrieved the extra coil of electrical wire and the needle nosed pliers he needed to cut and bare the wire. He admired the workmanship of the newer timing devices, which were only recently available. The word on the street was that an Irish priest had procured them from a Belgium supplier. He removed his glasses and wiped the sweat from his forehead with the perfumed linen handkerchief a woman had left in his room the night before in Belfast. He sniffed the handkerchief and grinned. He had never thought of himself as an attractive man and didn't give a tinker's damn one way or the other. There was nothing a few pounds wouldn't buy. Paying for his women was less complicated and saved a lot of time and effort. If a woman pleased him he was generous to a fault, and the few that didn't he got rid of in short order. Tomorrow night he would be back in Belfast and after a few hours sleep and a good supper he would find himself an attractive woman. After tonight he deserved something special.

The road was deserted as the lorry started the long slow climb up the steep, winding road towards Ballycastle. Meagher found the package of Woodbines on the empty seat beside him and lit another cigarette. He was satisfied with the night's work so far. They'd been lucky, all the same. It could just as easily have gone badly wrong in Bushmills or at Ballintoy harbour for that matter. It had taken months for an IRA veteran, living in New York, to locate an arms' supplier who could supply what was needed, and almost as long to arrange for a boat to drop the shipment at the small remote harbour on the Antrim coast. Tonight's arms shipment was only the beginning. Plans were already underway, he knew, to ship a large quantity of AK-18 and AK-15 Armalite assault rifles from New York via Southampton onboard the Queen Elizabeth II.

The Wicklow man taped the timer and detonator to the explosive bundle, checked the wiring and carefully placed the device in a large canvas bag. The timer would be set only when Meagher gave the word; it was something they had agreed upon from the beginning. They were not about to blow themselves up like the poor buggers in Belfast who were killed when the bomb they were carrying exploded as their car approached Donegale Square. He reached into the larger of the three wooden crates and unwrapped an AR-18 from its protective covering. Opening one of the smaller crates he retrieved two clips of ammunition. He clipped one into the AR-18 as Meagher had ordered, and placed the weapon and the extra clip of ammunition on the narrow wooden seat beside him. He felt uncomfortable handling the weapon and, as an afterthought, pushed it well out of reach. The Wicklow man carried a pistol, but only out of necessity. The truth was he had little stomach for using it. He was content to leave the shooting to the cold hearted bastard who sat only a few feet in front of him. For now his work was done. After a few minutes, he leaned back against the side of the lorry and moments later went to sleep, but not before thinking again of the woman in Belfast who had given him so much pleasure the night before.

Chapter Four

Inside the police barracks Sergeant Paddy Troy poured himself a mug of hot tea from a china teapot and returned to his desk by the window overlooking the street. The rain and fog had settled in for the evening leaving the street outside deserted. His arthritis was bothering him more than usual lately and he was thankful to be indoors on such a damp miserable night. Paddy Troy was a thirty year veteran of the Ulster Constabulary and although there was nothing particularly distinguished about his long career, he was a respected and well liked member of the small seaside community he called his home. He belonged to the Church of Ireland and had served on the parish vestry for the last ten years. He'd not planned to be on vestry that long, but they kept asking him to stay on and he never quite found a way to say no. Since his wife's death he had devoted more and more of his spare time to the church and to working with children from the local orphanage home. For the most part, he was content with his life and happily reconciled himself to the fact that he would retire in Ballycastle on a sergeant's pension. It was more than enough to get by on and for that he was grateful. The town was a pleasant place to live and he had no desire to be anywhere else, especially now. His young wife, he remembered fondly, had fallen in love with the place the first time she laid eyes on it. A few years before her illness they had saved up enough money to buy a small house of their own overlooking the sea. From their front window they could see Fair Head and Rathlin Island. And on a bright day the coast of Scotland was visible on the distant horizon. They had shared a good life together and by his reckoning they were more fortunate than most. All the same, there was so much more they'd planned to do, but in the end it wasn't to be.

He had worked hard to support their only son who would finish medical school in the spring. Already he was busy making plans to attend the graduation ceremony at Trinity College. He thought he might hire a car and drive to Dublin. He'd not done that before and the more he turned it over in his mind, the more he was beginning to warm up to the idea. That way they could drive back home together, see a bit of the country as well, and have a great yarn on the journey. A few weeks earlier he had tried on a well tailored navy blue suit in Tweedy Acheson's in Coleraine, but at the last minute decided against it. Now he was having second thoughts; maybe, he should buy the new suit after all. The graduation would be a grand affair and it seemed only right that he should look his best for it wasn't everyday a man's son graduated from the university. It was something for an old man to remember and take pleasure in long after the event had passed.

He drank a mouthful of hot tea and set the mug down. A framed black and white photograph that was beginning to fade around the edges sat on the wooden desk in front of him. It was a picture of a young woman in a light summer frock and a large sun hat sitting on a rock by the seaside. The dress, he remembered, was brown with large white polka dots and it suited her so well. It gave him pleasure to see her wear it. He remembered too, that she had kept it for a long time, long after it was too small for her to wear. The picture had been taken at Castlerock a few months after they were married. Picking it up he gently traced the outline of her face with his finger as if reaching out to touch her. That was how he would always remember her, just the way she looked in the photograph on that warm summer afternoon so long ago.

In the end the cancer destroyed her and it broke his heart to see her go that way. Somehow it didn't seem right that she should suffer the way she did and for so long, and for awhile he blamed God and then himself for not taking better care of her. In time his anger left him but the pain remained. Some days were better than others, but as the years passed he came to accept that too. "Ooh, I miss you, love, God knows I do..." he said softly, as he carefully placed the picture back on the desk directly in front of him. Now more than ever, he wished she were here so that together they might share one another's joy in their son's achievement. She would be so proud of him. She'd not been to Dublin either, he recalled. A pity, for she would have enjoyed the trip down and back. It was a place they had often talked about visiting, but like so many other things they just never managed to get around to it. Tomorrow he was off and would make a point of visiting the grave just for a quiet chat.

He reached for the mug of tea and for the second time that evening scanned the Coleraine Chronicle. After a few minutes he lost interest in the paper and returned to the letter he had started writing earlier in the evening. He had never been much of a letter writer, but somehow it seemed more important now that his wife was gone. It was what she would have done. The large wall clock above his head struck nine o'clock. Constable Burns would be back off patrol within the hour, perhaps even sooner, and with any luck they would both manage to get home at a reasonable hour. Stretching his arms above his head he yawned wearily; he wasn't feeling himself lately, but he was certain it was nothing a good night's sleep wouldn't cure. Then too, he was not as young as he used to be and had to admit, with some misgivings, that over the last few years he had noticed a need to occasionally doze off at the end of a long shift.

At Coolkenny, the Land-Rover turned slowly onto the main road and headed back towards Ballycastle. Constable Burns was happy in his work and like most young men his age enjoyed sitting behind the wheel of a powerful motor car. It was one of the things he liked about policing rural Ireland and he much preferred the work to walking the beat in one of the larger urban centres of the province, even if the weather in this part of the country was not always to his liking. It had not taken him long to realize that in winter it was often bitterly cold along the coast and the raw winds that blew in from the sea carried sheets of stinging rain that went right through you in a matter of minutes. The Rover wasn't built for comfort, but it kept him out of the weather. Like most nights the patrol had been uneventful. Traffic on the road was light and he only left the vehicle once to assist an elderly motorist who had taken the wrong road out of Armoy.

A native of county Fermanagh, Constable Burns had spent most of his young life growing up in the town of Enniskillen. He was a long way from home and the recent troubles made it difficult for him to see his family on a regular basis. Still, things were looking up. A few weeks ago he met a girl at a dance in Portrush and before the evening was over they'd agreed to see each other again. He touched the brake lightly as the Land-Rover entered a patch of heavy fog. She was a big soft girl with laughing eyes. His uncle had told him once that a big soft Irish girl was hard to beat. He was right. Next time he might even muster up enough courage to kiss her goodnight. He touched the brake again, harder this time, and the front of the Rover tipped down then rose again as he eased his foot back on the accelerator.

Sergeant Troy neatly folded the short letter he had just finished writing to his son and placed it in an envelope along with the two new ten pound notes he had taken out of his savings account earlier in the day. He sealed the envelope and placed it in his tunic pocket. It would be mailed first thing in the morning as soon as the post office opened. Yawning, he rose to his feet and walked down the hallway into the small room that served as a kitchen. He washed his mug and rinsed out the teapot with hot water from the kettle that was whistling on the gas cooker beside him. Reaching up he took down a package of tea from the small cupboard above the sink and emptied two large teaspoons into the china teapot and filled it with boiling water. Young Burns was fond of his tea too and would enjoy a hot mug especially tonight. He wiped the small tiled counter top with a damp dishcloth, placed a clean mug and teaspoon on the counter and walked back to his desk at the front of the building. Sergeant Troy glanced at the wall clock. It was almost twenty five minutes past nine.

A mile west of the town the rain eased to a steady drizzle. The fog was still thick in places, but better than it had been a few miles back. Behind the steering wheel Meagher listened to the monotonous sound of tires rolling on the wet pavement; it was a familiar sound to a man who was often alone on the road in the middle of the night. Terrorism had become a way of life and with it the realization he was destined to spend his life on the run always looking over his shoulder and never completely trusting anyone. His mind quickly returned to the road ahead as the lorry slowed and eased into a secluded churchyard just off the main road. He switched off the headlamps, reached back and tapped the small window behind the seat. The Wicklow man was already awake and quickly rechecked the wiring on the timing device before placing the explosives back in the canvas bag. He pushed the bag to the back of the lorry, picked up the assault rifle and the extra clip of ammunition and joined the other man in the front of the lorry. Climbing into the passenger's seat he handed Meagher the AR-18.

Minutes later they entered the quiet town of Ballycastle.

The street was deserted as the lorry coasted to a stop just beyond the large electric lantern illuminating the front of the police barracks. The fog and drizzle combined to create a halo of light that hung suspended above the entrance and cast a soft pool of reflected light on the wet street below. Both men stepped down onto the pavement in silence. Meagher turned and pointed to the back of the lorry. The small man nodded and moved quickly to retrieve the bomb. As he did so he uttered a silent Hail Mary. For him this was always the most difficult part, the place where a man could drown without anyone knowing he had slipped under the water. It was a bad place to be and the shooting only made it worse. At the beginning when he first joined the organization it wasn't like that. You blew the odd thing up and got the hell out before anyone was any the wiser. Now all that had changed and he didn't like it one bloody bit. Meagher reached into the cab, grabbed the AR-18 and the extra clip of ammunition and motioned to the entrance.

"Now."

"Oh, Jasus...."

"Hurry."

Sergeant Paddy Troy flushed the lavatory and started back towards the office. He thought he'd heard someone knocking on

62

the heavy wooden door, but he couldn't be certain. Now, there was no mistaking it. "Who in God's name could that be at this hour of the night?" he muttered, as he walked towards the door and looked through the tiny glass window. The man standing on the other side of the door was a British Army soldier. Sergeant Troy hesitated for a moment to regain his composure and then unlocked the door.

Meagher waited just long enough for the door to open, then, in a split second, raised the assault rifle, firing a burst into the large overweight man who stood directly in front of him. The AR-18 caught the sergeant across the chest reeling him backwards against the wall. His head slumped forward and he slid to the floor leaving a trail of blood smeared on the wall behind him. There was no need for a second burst. The Wicklow man stepped hurriedly over the body and made his way to a small room near the centre of the hallway. He set the timing device and immediately started back towards the street. Meagher looked at the dead man lying at his feet as the other man hurriedly moved towards the door. He stepped back, drew the service revolver from his pocket, and shot him through the head.

"Bastard!" The Wicklow man stammered, as he reached the door.

"Get out, now!" Meagher, shouted angrily

"Jasus, you didn't have to do that."

"Now, damn you."

Constable Burns couldn't be certain, but he thought he heard the sound of automatic fire as the Land-Rover started down the hill into the middle of the town. He accelerated along the deserted street and brought the Land-Rover to an abrupt halt a short distance behind a motor lorry parked a few feet beyond the front entrance. He had almost run into the back of it and had only seen it just in the nick of time. The lorry was now visible in his headlights and from where he sat he could see the British Army insignia on the tailgate. It didn't make any sense; maybe he had been mistaken. Then he noticed the front door to the barracks was wide open. Reaching for his revolver he nervously stepped down from his vehicle onto the road. As he did so he heard the sound of a revolver being fired from somewhere inside the building, and a moment later a man in uniform ran through the open door into the street.

"Stop, police...."

But it was already too late. As the Wicklow man reached the street he stumbled into the glare of two powerful headlights. Panic stricken, he fired wildly at the blinding lights, extinguishing one of the headlamps.

"Oh, Jesus...please stop."

Constable Burns raised his revolver and fired two rounds in the direction of the small man who had now turned back towards the entrance.

The Wicklow man heard a crashing sound, the loudest he had ever known, and for a fleeting second experienced a sickening feeling in the pit of his stomach. The rain and fog engulfed him until he was no longer aware of anything. Part of his skull had been blown away by the large calibre bullet that caught him in the back of the head. He lay face down on the wet street and for a few brief desperate moments, his hands and feet jerked uncontrollably as if trying to hold onto life. The Wicklow man was dead.

Meagher had almost reached the door when he heard the exchange of gun fire on the street.

"Christ! What now?"

Instinctively he sprang backwards and made his way into the small kitchen at the end of the hallway. He reached up and switched off the electric light bulb hanging from the ceiling.

Constable Burns stood in the rain looking down at the body of the man who lay on the pavement.

"Oh, dear God...what have I done?"

For the first time in his young life he had shot and killed a man. Nothing in his two years of service with the Royal Ulster Constabulary had prepared him for this.

"Why didn't you stop....Oh, Jesus, why didn't you stop?"

Breathing deeply, he tried to steady himself against the side of the Land-Rover. For God's sake, man, get a hold of yourself, he whispered, as he staggered forward and stepped cautiously through the lighted doorway into the hallway. Sergeant Troy lay on the floor a short distance down the hall, his tunic saturated in blood from the gaping wound across his chest. He started to tremble and again reached out to steady himself. "Oh Jesus." His eyes clouded as he looked at the man, who in the course of a few short months had become his friend. He had never seen a man die this way. There was so much blood.

"Oh, sweet Jesus... Help me."

He fell against the wall gasping for breath, trying desperately to regain control. He felt his stomach heave and he knew he was going to vomit. His arms fell to his side and he relaxed his grip on the revolver. He saw the man emerge from the shadows holding an automatic weapon.

"Ooh, no...."

Slowly, he raised his revolver as the soldier opened fire.

Constable Burns fell backwards through the open door into the halo of vanishing light.

Meagher looked anxiously at his watch. Damn it, there's always the unexpected, he thought, as he moved quickly towards the entrance. Outside on the street he saw the Wicklow man lying on the wet pavement. The drizzle was again turning to rain as Meagher reached down and picked up the pistol that was lying on the ground just beyond the Wicklow man's outstretched arm.

"You stupid bastard," Meagher said, slowly shaking his head at the small man lying at his feet, "you never had the stomach for it, did you?"

He turned and walked away without looking back.

A moment later, the lorry pulled out into the street that would take him directly through the town and back onto the main road. Meagher reached for the pack of Woodbines and hurriedly lit a cigarette. He needed a smoke badly. Settling back in the seat he inhaled deeply and waited for the sound of an explosion. If the Wicklow man had done his job he would not have to wait long. Easing his grip on the steering wheel Meagher felt the first signs of weariness. The heavy rain and poor visibility only added to his fatigue. He would be glad to put this night behind him. In a matter of minutes the lorry passed the Golf Links on the outskirts of Ballycastle.

Behind him there was a loud explosion that shook buildings all along the street and filled the night air with flying glass and debris. Meagher nodded. The Wicklow man had done his job after all. But sure he had always done his job, however much he may have disliked what he had to do. It was then it occurred to him that he would be hard to replace. Aye, well that's for another day, he thought, as the lorry headed inland towards Ballyvoy and the road that would take him over the mountain to the small fishing village of Cushendun on the northeast coast. In this weather the journey would take longer than he had anticipated. He knew too, that within hours security forces would be mobilized and the longer he stayed on the road the greater the risk of detection. By morning, the Army would discover that one of their vehicles had been stolen.

On the other side of the street, opposite the police barracks, a young woman unable to move, cried out for help. Just beyond her reach a small child lay bleeding on the wet pavement.

Chapter Five

Inside Doherty's pub the smell of stale whiskey hung in the damp air. A small coal fire burned in an open fireplace. Thompson removed his cap and overcoat and threw them over the back of an empty chair. Wiping the rain from his neck and forehead with a dry handkerchief he moved closer to the fire and rubbed his hands together to help restore the circulation. He stood by the fire for several minutes before reaching into his overcoat pocket for the pack of Gallaghers he had bought earlier in the day. He lit a cigarette, inhaled deeply, and stared at the ornate plaster ceiling above his head. It had recently been painted for he was able to pick out a pattern on the plaster work he hadn't noticed before. Other than that, the room looked the same; it was one of the things he liked about the place, nothing much ever changed, including the people who came for a quiet drink on a Saturday night. He turned from the fire and sat down in an empty chair by the window overlooking the street. Reaching across the table he picked up the glass of Irish whiskey the older Doherty had brought him a few minutes earlier.

For a time he sat in silence listening contentedly to the sound of rain beating against the small glass window panes. A sudden gust of wind rattled and shook the wooden window frame, then retreated, leaving only the sound of rain against the window. Outside on the street there was a distant rumble of thunder and Thompson surrendered to the stream that carried him to an earlier time, to a time of hope and innocence, and carefree abandonment. Again he remembered his father and their walks together on a Sunday morning up the Mountsandel Road or along the abandoned railway track that followed the river and ran from the harbour to the railway station. He recalled too, the old barge lying half submerged by the railway bridge where his father told him it was from this very spot that he first swam across the Bann. And on one of these walks he once told his father that if he hadn't got married and there was only the two of them they would have a car by now. His father had told his mother and she had replied that it didn't say much for her.

Sometimes, on longer walks, they crossed the river and set off along Waterside and the Strand, walking as far as the Salmon Leap. It was a long way for a little boy. His father must have thought so too for often he picked him up in his arms and set him on his shoulders when he was too tired to walk any farther. And from this vantage point, he could see the whole world, or at least as much of it as he cared to see. All the while they had some grand chats about his father's life, the things he'd done and the places he'd seen. And sometimes his father talked about his own modest hopes for the future, but more often than not, he talked about his children and how important it was to get a good education if you were going to get on in life. He just wanted his children to have a better chance than he had. That's what he remembered most about his father.

When the weather grew warmer they often spent Sunday afternoon together wandering through the Anderson Park or sitting on one of the freshly painted park benches that were painted a lovely shade of green. Sometimes he set off with his younger brother to explore the dark secrets of the park or to hide from their father as he sat on a bench leisurely reading the

Sunday paper and smoking one of his cigarettes. And later when they became thirsty from running around in the warm afternoon sun, they ran across Circular Road to the park on the other side of the road and drank cold water from iron cups that were chained to the cast iron bowl of the Anderson fountain. He recalled his father telling him that when he was a boy playing in the park, he too drank from the same iron cups that were now worn smooth as glass by the hands of countless children. And afterwards he thought about that for a long time. His father also told him that in 1899 a man called Hugh Anderson donated a substantial sum of money to lay out a public park on land that had been offered to the town a few years earlier. The park and the fountain were named for the Anderson family.

As he grew older he came to realize how much his father knew about all kinds of things. For a working man with little formal education, his father knew a great deal about the town and its long history as one of the earliest inhabited sites in Ireland. It was from his father he first learned that it was probably St. Patrick who gave the town its name. Legend had it, his father told him, that when St. Patrick visited the local area he was offered a piece of ground on which to build a church, the very site where Saint Patrick's stands today. The area was covered in ferns and many believed the name Coleraine was derived from *cuil rathain,* the Irish phrase used by St. Patrick to describe the area, meaning ferny corner.

And on another occasion when they stopped briefly to listen to the Salvation Army Band playing at an open air meeting he learned something else from his father he hadn't known before. His father remarked jokingly that the Army had nothing on St. Patrick for the patron Saint of Ireland had long ago conducted open air services at Mountsandel.

When the weather permitted, he and his younger brother occasionally travelled with their father by bus or train to visit other places not far from Coleraine, places that were a special

69

part of his father's life, places he wanted his children to know about so that they too would have a sense of belonging and a connection with family that they had only heard about or seen in an old faded family photograph. Through the eyes of a young boy he saw the wonder and beauty of the Ireland his father loved, the awesome sight of a gathering storm swept inland by the powerful winds of the North Atlantic, the rugged beauty of the small village of Downhill with its towering cliffs rising vertically above the narrow coastal road. He remembered too, the smooth golden sand of Magilligan Strand that stretched as far as the eye could see, and beyond in the distance, the Irish Free State and green purple hills of Donegal rising out of the dark waters of Lough Foyle - a solitude, broken only by the sound of wind and the relentless ocean.

Time passed.

A wooden coin box rattled beside him and he turned abruptly to stare at the small plump middle aged woman in a Salvation Army uniform who squinted through her thick glasses and pointed at the collection box with a short fat stabbing finger. She startled him and he glared back at the woman almost in anger. The box rattled again, this time louder than before, and he knew from past experience she was not about to move on until she received a contribution, however small, to support the Army's work. Out of habit, he reached into his trousers pocket and retrieving a two shilling piece placed it in the small box in front of him. Nodding, he dismissed the woman and reaching across the table took a small drink of whiskey from the glass that was now almost empty. Annie Quinn was no stranger to him or to anyone else who frequented public houses in Coleraine on a regular basis. She was a pitiful soul who evoked a kind of sympathy and tolerance from everyone who knew her. Annie had been a member of the Salvation Army for as long as he could remember and her weekly visits to public houses, in the company of other Salvationists, made her a permanent fixture in

70

pubs throughout the borough. She was to be seen too, tirelessly shaking her wooden box in people's faces as she worked the queues lining up to see a picture at Christie's or the Palladium.

He debated briefly with himself as to whether or not he should have another, although the truth was it wasn't much of a debate for a moment later he caught Doherty's eye and raised his glass "The same?"

"Aye."

The sound of a small concertina filled the room and a familiar tenor voice began to sing from a worn evangelical song book.

I'd rather have Jesus, than silver or gold;
I'd rather have him, than have mansions untold.
I'd rather have Jesus, than houses or lands;
I'd rather be led by his nailed pierced hand....

Thompson turned and stared at the tall balding tenor standing erect in a Salvation Army uniform. He had known Bobbie Corbett from the time they had worked together as apprentice bricklayers to a local contractor building council houses a few miles outside the town. As he watched, Bobbie closed his eyes and sang the last verse.

He's fairer than lilies of rarest bloom;
He's sweeter than honey from out the comb.
He's all that my hungering spirit needs;
I'd rather have Jesus and let him lead
Than to be the king of a vast domain,
Or be held in sins dread sway;
I'd rather have Jesus than anything,
This world affords today.

When the song ended, Bobbie stood motionless, his head and eyes raised in homage and praise to the God he had come to know and love. The pub was silent.

Thompson turned away and gazed into the open fire. Bobbie's singing always moved him. He had a great way with a song when he put his heart into it, and his heart was in it tonight he thought, nodding his head in silent approval.

Bobbie Corbett was a reformed alcoholic and a born again Christian. He still lived with his family in the small stone house at the bottom of Brook Street not far from where he was born. Each day he rode his bicycle to work as he had done all his life. But he was a changed man, a change that was plain enough to see especially by those who had known him before his conversion. He was at peace with himself and the world around him. You could see it in his eyes. Thompson picked up his glass and took a long slow drink of whiskey.

The silence was broken by a round of applause as a drunk staggered to his feet to shake Bobbie's hand. It was somebody Bobbie knew and he reached out and took his hand. And from somewhere across the room an old woman hollered out."Ah, God love you Bobbie, God love you, son."

Bobbie smiled and waved at the old woman. He knew most of them, especially the older crowd. "Aye, and he loves you too, Nelly."

"Bobbie, your oull mother would be proud of you....you're one of us son."

"I am."

"Och God love you son.... sing us another song."

The place fell silent again at the sound of the concertina. Bobbie looked around the crowded smoke filled room and smiling began to sing.

The chimes of time ring out the news, another day is through,
Someone slipped and fell, was that someone you
You may have longed for added strength, your courage to
renew, do not be discouraged, I have news for you.

It is no secret, what God can do
What He's done for others, He'll do for you
With arms wide open, He'll pardon you
It is no secret what God can do....

He sang only the first verse and the chorus. When he finished the last line he bowed his head in silent prayer. This time there was no applause. Bobbie clasped his hands together and standing as erect as before shared his testimony of how one night in a public house just like this one his life had been miraculously transformed by the power of the risen Jesus. His sins he said had been washed away by the blood of the Lamb, and from that moment on he was freed from his addiction. Smiling again he told them he had received his BA and an MA - born again and made anew. What the Saviour had done for him he was willing do for them....all they had to do, he said, his voice full of emotion, was simply to believe in the Lord Jesus Christ and accept him into their hearts as their personal Saviour and God will do the rest.

In the far corner of the pub, sitting in the shadows, a well dressed middle aged man fondled a young woman who had had too much to drink. She giggled softly and pulled her dress down over her knees as she caught Thompson's eye. The man said something to her and she giggled again. Thompson looked at the young woman for a moment, and then returned his gaze to the open fire.

"Boys o' boys, Willie, that's a bad oull night", Bobbie Corbett said, looking down at Thompson who was still gazing into the hearth.

"Och, sure, the weather's powerful for this time of the year," Thompson replied, looking up at the tall balding man who was now standing beside the table.

"Ah, you're looking rightly, Willie, for a'oull fella your age."

"Aye, and you too, Bobbie, you too.... Sure you don't look a day older since I saw you down the street this morning."

Bobbie smiled. He was fond of Thompson and had always enjoyed his sense of humour. Many an evening they'd frittered away together, foolishly spending what little hard earned money they had drinking whiskey and porter, sometimes so drunk at the end of the night they couldn't ride their bicycles home. That was a long time ago, Bobbie thought, as he looked at his old friend resting heavily against the back of his chair. He wasn't drunk, he could see that, but he'd probably had enough. He wanted to say something, but thought better of it for he knew in his heart his old friend wouldn't listen.

"Who's the wee fella with you Bobbie?" Thompson asked, pointing to the young man wearing a dark brown suit and a Salvation Army cap who was standing in the corner talking to the young woman Thompson had been watching a few moments earlier.

"That's Harry Park's wee boy. Sure you may remember the father, and the mother as well. The mother's still living in the town in a wee house in Taylor's Row."

Thompson shook his head in disbelief. "Ah, go away with yourself. I never knew oull Harry had a son that age."

"Aye, and an older one than that too."

"You don't say."

"I do...."

"Tell me Bobbie, wasn't oull Harry drowned at the bar mouth a few years back, in some sort of boating accident? I don't think they ever found him."

"Aye, he was...he was indeed, Willie. And a sad day it was too, leaving a wife and two sons to get by as best they could. The mother went to work and managed to raise the two boys without much help from anyone."

"Well, I'll tell you one thing, the mother should be proud of that wee fella. We could do with a few more like him."

Turning to look at the young man, Bobbie smiled and nodded

74

in agreement. "God knows that's the truth." He paused for a moment before continuing. "Aye, the mother's proud of him right enough....sure we all are. To hear him speak you'd hardly believe he's only a young fellow. I heard him speak at the Salvation Army in Ballymoney, and I'll tell you, I was moved by what he had to say. A man could learn from a wee fellow like that."

"Aye...true enough."

"Well tell me, Willie, are you in good form yourself?" Bobbie asked.

"Och, as well as can be expected, Bobbie. This oull damp weather doesn't help th'oull rheumatism," Thompson said, rubbing his bad leg lightly with his hand. "Sometimes it's better than others, but it always seems to be worse this time of the year. I don't think there's much they can do for it and if there is it's a well kept secret."

"It's a common enough complaint."

"Aye, I suppose it is living in a country like this. Mind you, other than that, they tell me, I'm as fit as a fiddle... if you can believe half of what they tell you."

Bobbie was smiling again."I'm glad to hear it and what about the rest of the family?"

"Ah, the very best, Bobbie, sure they're all doing well. The eldest boy's a priest now. You remember Podraic, the one you always said was blessed with his mother's good looks."

"Aye, I do...I do."

"Molly's back living here now and Aggie the younger sister is still in school. Bertie's across the water and doing well for himself. He was home just a few weeks ago and by the look of him I reckon he's happy enough where he is. I wouldn't think we'll see him back living in Ireland anytime soon."

"And how is the wife?"

"Och, just the same, Bobbie, Mary never changes from one day to the next. She's a wonderful woman and always on the go. I don't think she knows how to say no. She's not getting any younger either, but it doesn't seem to bother her one bit."

"Boys o' boys, you'd hardly believe where the time goes, it seems no time since they were all in school," Bobbie said, shaking his head. He knew both the Thompson boys and over the years had watched them grow into fine young men. The two girls he knew only to see on the street.

"Aye, right enough, Bobbie, sure time flies."

"You have much to be thankful for Willie."

"Aye... I do, Bobbie. And the business is doing well too, I have a good bunch of men working for me, and so I'm able to come and go these days more or less as I please. There seems to be lots of work in Coleraine for the small building contractor."

Bobbie nodded, "aye, that seems to be the case." He turned to leave, but before he did, he reached across the table and tapped Thompson on the shoulder, "Remember now, God's not that far away, even in the case of a'oull rascal like yourself...God knows, I ought to know."

Thompson smiled, but took little heed.

"Good night, Bobbie..."

"Aye, and good night to you Willie"

He watched the small group of Salvationists gather up their belongings and head for the door. It was then that he noticed that one of the usual crowd was absent. It was Billy McCloskey who lived on the outskirts of the town, a man addicted to drink, whose life was transformed one night, at a Salvation Army meeting in Long Commons, many years ago. He was a gentle soft spoken man who worked with his two sons painting cars and vans in a small rented garage not far from where he lived. Billy had a good word to say about everybody and it didn't seem to bother him how hard he had to work to keep his family going. That's probably why he's not here tonight, Thompson thought, he's likely finishing up a rush job for someone who needs the van on the road on Monday morning. It was Bobbie who told him that Billy couldn't read and always relied on the two boys to make sure the words he was lettering on the side of the van were spelled correctly. Most of the time he got it right, but once in awhile he made a mistake if one of the boys wasn't there to write out the letters of the words beforehand. Nothing much seemed to bother him and if it did he never complained. He had known him for a long time, almost as long as he'd known Bobbie Corbett.

When the last of the group had gone, he was again conscious of the wind and the rain striking the window panes and by the sound of it he reckoned he was in for another miserable walk across the Bann. Making his way home on a bad night was always the worst part of it and he often reproached himself for not having the good sense to stay home.

Doherty placed the glass of Old Bushmills on the table and returned to his stool behind the bar. Thompson stared at the glass of whiskey and for a time his thoughts turned again to Bobbie Corbett and Long Commons. He took a long, slow drink of whiskey, then, carefully set the glass back down on the table, turning it in his hand as he did so. He sat in silence studying the glass for a moment trying to make up his mind whether it was half empty or half full

Reaching for the packet of Gallaghers and the box of matches, he lit another cigarette and threw the match into the fire. A short time later he finished his whiskey and pushing the chair back from the table got to his feet and for a few minutes stood in front of the open fire, enjoying what warmth was left in the dying coals. It was time to go home.

He pulled on his cap and overcoat and made his way to the door that led to the street.

"Mind how you go, then," he heard the older Doherty say as he reached the door.

Thompson nodded. "Aye.... I'll do that."

Chapter Six

The old priest stared at the empty bottle of Jamieson's on the small round mahogany table beside him. His body swayed gently as he tried to pull himself upright in the chair. He had been drinking for the better part of the evening and his supper which had been prepared a few hours earlier sat untouched on the table beside the empty bottle of whiskey. His spectacles and two worn volumes of Irish poetry lay scattered about on the worn carpet at his feet. Earlier on, while he was still sober, he had read aloud a few of his favourite poems by Thomas Moore. *The Scent of the Roses*, like so many of Moore's poems had been set to music. It was one of his favourites and he liked the last verse so much that he often sang it just for the pleasure of it. He had a grand voice for a man of his years and enjoyed singing alone or even in the company of others although the opportunity rarely presented itself anymore. But mostly, now that he was older, he was content to sit in front of the fire and sing quietly to himself. The last few lines of the song moved him deeply and sometimes brought tears to his eyes, especially when he was drinking, as he was tonight. For a few moments he turned the familiar words over in his head and then began to sing in a low melancholy voice:

Long, long be my heart with such memories fill'd!
Like the vase, in which roses have once been distill'd -
You may break, you may shatter the vase, if you will,
But the scent of the roses will hang round it still....

The old man's eyes watered as he picked up the bottle and turned it slowly upside down to drain the last few drops of whiskey into the glass sitting on the table. His hand shook and the few drops of precious whiskey that were left in the bottle spilled onto the table. Wiping his brow with the sleeve of his soiled cassock the bottle slipped from his hand and fell to the floor.

Father Nolan was drunk.

He looked up at the clock on the mantelpiece as it struck ten. His head fell backwards on the high backed armchair as he fumbled in his pocket for the packet of Players the housekeeper had brought him earlier in the afternoon. The effort proved too much for him and he decided against trying again. It was hardly worth the bother he reasoned, and besides, in his present state, there was always the chance he might set himself or the house on fire. You old fool, he thought, you'll never learn. God knows that's the truth, but what can a man do when all is said and done. He was quick to acknowledge his shortcomings but that was as far as it went for he had no great inclination to change his ways at this stage in his life. Many a good man, even a man of the cloth, needed a drop or two now and again to see him through, and sure what's the harm in it, for wasn't drinking a glass of good whiskey one of the few civilized customs left in Ireland. It wasn't for everyone, that much he acknowledged. For one thing, a man needed time to drink, but sure time was something he had plenty of. Maybe that's why I'm drunk so often. I've too much time on my hands, he mused, as he ran his finger through the tiny pool of whiskey on the stained mahogany table. He raised the finger to his mouth and licked the end of it with his tongue. "How did that oull poem go, ah sure, I remember now."

Why, liquor of life! do I love you so;
When in all our encounters you lay me so low?
More stupid and senseless I every day grow,
What a hint...if I'd mend by the warning....

He raised his eyebrows creating deep furrows in his weathered forehead as he tried to remember the rest of the words. "I'm damned if I can remember, ah, never mind," he grunted, as he tried again to sit upright in the chair. The rest of his body ignored him and he slumped back down into the chair, a defeated, but happy man, nonetheless.

At that moment, the housekeeper burst into the room. "Father, you haven't eaten a bite of your supper. And didn't I buy that lovely wee piece of steak just for you. God only knows why I bother!" she shouted, throwing her hands in the air.

"I can see you're none too pleased, Mrs Cassidy."

"Aye, and small wonder."

Despairingly, she wiped her hands on her apron and without taking her eyes off him reached over and gathered up the supper plate. Ignoring the whiskey bottle on the floor, she reached down and picked up his spectacles from the carpet at his feet.

"Ah, would you look at the sight of yourself."

"Och, I can't look that bad."

"Worse."

"Och, away with you."

"You should see yourself, that is, if you can still see."

"I can see well enough to see the likes of you."

"I'm surprised you can see at all."

"Och, would you leave me in peace."

"I'll do no such thing. You're a disgrace, that's what you are," she said, shaking her head in anger. "You'd think an oull man your age would have more sense. God forgive me for saying it." "Mind your tongue, Mrs Cassidy."

"I'll do no such thing. Would you look at yourself? Sure you're full of th'oull drink again."

"Aye, well, I'll tell you a wee thing, Mrs Cassidy, I'll be sober in the morning, but you'll still be a contrary oull woman."

"God help me, to think you'd say the likes of that to an oull woman like myself who's worked her fingers to the bone day in and day out trying to look after you and that's the thanks I get. I'm the bigger fool for putting up with you all these years. God forgive me for saying it, but you'd try the patience of a saint, you would."

"I wouldn't have thought you knew any."

"Go on, say what you like. I'm leaving anyway. I've done all I care to do around here for one night. I'm for my own bed and none too soon after listening to the likes of you. And you'd be wise to do the same if you can still stand on the two feet God gave you," she hollered.

"Aye, well, off you go, and good riddance."

"The devil himself could do nothin' with you," she added, as she left the room in a huff, muttering away to herself as she went.

"Mind how you go then, it's fit for neither man nor beast out there tonight." Or cheeky oull women he almost shouted after her, but thought better of it. God knows, it wouldn't take much to get her started again.

After a few minutes he heard the front door slam behind her. That woman's got a bad tongue in her mouth, he thought, and a temper to go with it. But he was fond of her just the same. He knew too, that no one else in the parish would have bothered to put up with him all these years. She meant well, and besides, if the truth were known, he enjoyed her wit and sharp tongue more than he was prepared to let on. Although, he had noticed lately she seemed more contrary than usual. A good stiff drink might do her the world of good. Thank God, priests are celibate, he thought; an oull woman like that would drive a man to drink in no time at all.

Father Nolan had been a parish priest for as long as he cared to remember. And although he had spent a good part of his life in the Republic of Ireland, mostly in small rural parishes, he had willingly returned to the six counties when requested by the Bishop to do so. He was seventy years old and in good health for a man his age. A remarkable achievement he was fond of saying for a man who drank and smoked as much as he did. Mrs Cassidy told him, on more than one occasion, that he must have been spared for a reason, but for the life of her she had no notion of what it might be. The Antrim coast suited his temperament for he had a great fondness for the sea and for the men who made their living from it. He admired their quiet strength, their rugged individualism and their capacity to cope with the trials and uncertainties of ordinary life. Life was not always kind to the men of the sea, for the sea was unforgiving and unpredictable in its moods. But they took it in their stride and got on with the business of living, however bitter the pill of their misfortune. Through it all, they never lost their sense of humour. He remembered reading somewhere that an Arran man once told Synge that a man who is not afraid of the sea will soon be drowned, for he will be going out on a day when he shouldn't, but we who are afraid of the sea are only drowned now and again. The Arran man reminded him of the Antrim fishermen for sometimes they too did not come home. And like himself they often drank too much. It was a common failing among the Irish and common enough in Cushendall.

A few of the older woman in the parish were less tolerant of his drinking and wrote a strongly worded letter to the Bishop asking him to deal with the matter with the utmost dispatch. The Bishop sent word back advising them that given the sensitivity of the matter he would personally undertake to deal with it in a timely, but discreet manner to avoid, if possible, any undue embarrassment to the community and, in particular, to the good ladies who had brought the matter to his attention. That was over a year ago. Some of the women said that the good Bishop, true to his word, had handled the affair so discreetly that nobody in the parish, including Father Nolan, was any the wiser. The men of Cushendall had a different explanation. The Bishop himself, it was rumoured, was partial to a wee glass of the good stuff.

The room was warm from the turf fire that burned in the open grate. Out of habit the old priest glanced up at the clock on the mantle. It was fifteen minutes past the hour. He struggled to keep his eyes open, but to no avail; his head fell gently forward and in a few minutes he was fast asleep. A short time later he stirred as the grandfather clock in the hall chimed fifteen minutes past the hour. He shifted his weight on the chair, found a more comfortable position, and soon he was again snoring peacefully, his old grey head gently rising and falling to the rhythm of his heavy breathing.

Chapter Seven

South of Ballypatrick forest the fog thickened as the lorry neared the coast. Behind the wheel, Meagher was beginning to tire, his eyes burned from cigarette smoke and the constant glare of the headlamps reflecting back in the fog. He rubbed both eyes gently with his hand trying to relieve his discomfort. It had been a long difficult drive, too bloody long, he thought, as he placed his hand back on the steering wheel and fixed his eyes on the road ahead. A few miles up the road the lorry slowed again, turned left onto a secondary road and proceeded toward the outskirts of Cushendun. He reached for a cigarette, but changed his mind and threw the pack on the seat beside him. Meagher rolled down his window and took a deep breath of the cold moist air. He could smell the sea and knew he was almost there. Five minutes later he crossed the bridge over the Glendun River. A few hundred yards up the road the lorry turned into a long narrow overgrown lane. He could hear branches slapping on the roof and sides of the lorry as he moved slowly down the lane and started to climb a small hill. At the end of the laneway there was an iron gate pulled to one side to allow a vehicle to pass. Meagher drove through the open gate into a large cobbled stone yard and brought the lorry to a standstill. The rain had finally stopped and through the fog he could see plainly enough the outline of a large farmhouse. A man had emerged from the lighted back porch and was making his way towards him. As he watched, the man seemed to hesitate for a moment as if trying to make up his mind about something. Meagher turned off the engine and reached for the pack of Willy Woodbines he had thrown on the seat a short time earlier. He lit a cigarette and waited. The other man had almost reached the lorry. As the man approach Meagher carefully placed the cigarette in the ashtray and slipped his hand into his overcoat pocket.

"Is it yourself Meagher?"

"Aye, none other," Meagher answered, releasing his grip on the revolver. "Good thing you spoke when you did," Meagher added, in a half hearted attempt at humour.

Tommy McCann wasn't amused. He'd had dealings with Meagher in the past and he didn't like him, not one bloody bit. For that matter, as far as he knew, there wasn't anyone in his own small group that did. He was a pushy bastard and deadly. At least he's on our side; better the devil you know than the one you don't, he thought, as he thrust his hand through the open window to shake Meagher's hand. It was merely a formality and not a gesture of friendship.

"Where's your man?" Tommy asked, staring at the empty seat and half expecting Meagher to say he was behind the lorry taking a piss.

"He's dead." Meagher said, stepping out of the lorry.

"Och, Jesus, man, don't tell me that," the other man shouted back in shocked disbelief.

"I just did. He's bloody well dead."

McCann's mouth dropped. He was badly shaken by what Meagher had just told him and angered by the matter of fact way he said it. If he felt anything at all, he sure as hell didn't show it. It was as if the Wicklow man's death was no longer any concern of his. "For God's sake man, how did it happen?"

"Does it matter?" Meagher replied coldly.

"It bloody well does to me... he was a friend for God's sake."

"Well, if you must know, the RUC put a bullet in his head."

"Jesus, I don't believe it..."

"Suit yourself...and there's something else you should know while you're at it."

"And what would that be?"

"It was his own bloody fault and you can tell that to the rest of them."

There was an awkward silence between the two men. The other man looked at the empty lorry, then back at Meagher and shook his head.

"There was nothing I could do...he ran into the street and took a bullet in the back of the head for his trouble. There wasn't a damned thing I could do."

"I never said there was."

"No... no you didn't, then, let's leave it at that. Nobody should be surprised that in this business, people die. And I'll tell you something else, careless people die more often. It's happened before and it'll happen again before this is all over....you can be certain of that. The Wicklow man got careless, that's all, and he's bloody well dead and there's not a damned thing any of us can do about it."

"Maybe so, but it's a bad turn of events just the same," McCann said, regaining some of his composure. "All the more reason to get you out of Ireland before morning."

Meagher nodded in agreement.

"You'd better have something to eat."

"Aye..."

"You've a long night ahead of you. Go on over to the house and warm yourself by the fire. There's food prepared for you in the kitchen."

"And the change of clothing?"

"It's all there, just as you asked. Go on with you now. I'll attend to things out here. There's not much time; we had expected you earlier."

Meagher thanked him and walked briskly across the yard to the lighted doorway. He would be glad of a bite to eat and even happier to get out of this bloody uniform.

He saw her as soon as he walked through the kitchen door. She hadn't changed a bit. How long had it been, he wasn't certain, but it was at least a year, perhaps longer, since their chance meeting in the Irish Republic. They had spent the night together in a small hotel in Howth, County Dublin. He had done things with her he had not done with another woman. He smiled as he looked at the tall sensuous woman standing against the wall. Her legs were spread slightly apart pulling her dress snugly about her thighs. She ran her hands through her long dark hair and looked directly at Meagher. Meagher saw her eyes follow him as he came towards her. He kissed her lightly on the cheek and she discreetly stroked the inside of his hand with her finger.

"It's a shame you're so late," she whispered in his ear. "Had you come earlier, you might have had my silk knickers down."

Meagher nodded and quickly withdrew his hand. Two men came in from the yard before he had a chance to reply. It was a lovely thought all the same, but it would have to wait. Angela, he knew, was not one for waiting. She would have it on with someone else and probably sooner rather than later. She was a beautiful woman and there was no shortage of men willing to give her what she wanted. One of the men who had entered the room went to the kitchen and brought Meagher a plate of hot food and a bottle of stout. The man set the plate down roughly on the table.

Meagher took off the heavy overcoat, threw it over a chair and sat down to eat his supper.

"Fetch the other one, we don't have much time." Angela said, turning to the man who had brought Meagher his supper.

The man looked at Meagher, then back at the woman. "Aye, fetch him, you say.... is that what you said?"

"You know damned well that's what I said."

"Aye, well, I would if I could, but he's not likely to be joining us....is he now?" the man said, glancing back at Meagher.

"What the hell are you talking about?"

"Why don't you ask your big man there?" he said bitterly, in a heavy Belfast accent.

The woman paled and started to say something, but Meagher cut her off sharply. "The Wicklow man's gone," he said, controlling a sudden burst of anger directed at the Belfast man.

"Gone... what do you mean he's gone?"

"He's bloody well dead."

"Dead?"

"Aye... shot on the street by the RUC in Ballycastle."

The Wicklow man was well liked by the Antrim crowd and Meagher knew it, but he wasn't his bloody keeper, no matter what they might think. He took a long drink of stout and went on with his meal.

"I've been told he was good at his job," she said, without looking at anyone in particular.

"As good as they come," Meagher said coldly.

"He'll be missed, then."

"Aye... I suppose he will."

A few minutes later the two men left and went back into the yard, leaving Meagher and the woman alone. He drank the last of the stout and pushed the empty plate to one side. He was tired, more tired than he'd been in a long time, and his back ached from sitting too long in an uncomfortable lorry. He looked at his watch and then at the woman. "It's time to get this show on the road," he said, rising from the table.

"You'll find everything you need on the bed," she said,

pointing to the room across the hall.

Meagher nodded.

"Well, almost everything," she added.

"I'll just have to manage as best I can then, won't I."

"You will..."

He pushed his chair under the table and walked towards the bedroom unbuttoning his tunic as he went. His change of clothing was laid out neatly on the bed just as she had said. He dressed quickly with the ease of one accustomed to wearing familiar attire. He put on a pair of black leather shoes and stood in front of the mirror. The metamorphosis was complete. The tall priest smiled at the familiar face in the mirror. "Well, Father, I think you'll do." He picked up a black overcoat and walked back across the hall into the kitchen.

"If I didn't know better I'd swear you were one of them."

"That's the general idea, my child."

Tommy McCann and the two men had returned to the house. They were eager to be on their way. "We're ready," McCann said impatiently, looking at the man standing in front of him in a black cassock and clerical collar. "Well, I'll be damned.... you certainly look the part, Meagher, I'll grant you that much by God."

Meagher raised his hand. "Bless all in this house, my son."

"This is no time for bloody theatrics." McCann was growing more impatient. "We haven't got all night to sit around here with our fingers up our arse."

Meagher ignored him.

McCann shook his head. God, that's one cool bastard, just the same, he thought, as he watched Meagher pull on the overcoat and casually light a cigarette.

"We're off, then."

"We are, and you're with me Meagher," Tommy said, "Angela will do what needs to be done here. Your two boys over there know what has to be done to get rid of the lorry. When they get through, the damn police will look a long time before they find it and by then it won't matter one way or the other."

"And the shipment?"

"It's already been transferred to the Humber. You'll see for yourself on the way out. The whole lot's concealed in the back of the hearse. Take my word for it there's no bloody way they will be any the wiser...we've had good luck in the past. And who the hell's going to stop a hearse with a coffin in the back unless they've been tipped off. I'll see to it that it's driven into Belfast first thing on Monday in time to catch the rest of the traffic entering the city at that hour of the morning."

Meagher nodded his approval. He was confident now that nothing had been left to chance. Nothing, at least, that he was aware of. McCann he knew had a lot of experience in handling this sort of thing and it showed. He could only hope that the other two men were as competent. He dismissed the thought. There was no reason to believe otherwise and besides that was somebody else's problem. The woman, he knew, would leave nothing to chance.

"I trust you'll have an uneventful crossing, Father," Angela said, in mild amusement. "You're booked on the late boat to Liverpool. When you arrive you'll be met as you leave the boat and taken to a safe house not far from the city. You're expected and they know what to look for. Tommy has everything else you'll need. Oh, and one more thing, the boat's running late, so I don't think you'll have any difficulty."

"I'm sure I won't."

"That's that, then...."

"Aye, I suppose it is, it's too bad I was late."

"Shame on you, Father."

"Come on for Christ's sake," he heard McCann shout from the doorway. Meagher followed the other man outside and across the yard into a large well lit shed. Inside was an immaculate black Humber Super Snipe with a long graceful bonnet. Meagher

91

rubbed his hand along the smooth dark finish. "Boys o! That's a lovely motor car."

"Aye, right enough, sure half the countryside's dying for a ride in her." McCann said, with a straight face.

Meagher laughed.

Tommy walked to the back of the Humber and opened the rear door of the hearse. "Look for yourself," he said. "There's not a hint of anything out of place."

Meagher shook his head; it was just as the other man said. "You know your business, McCann," he said, and turned back towards the door. On the way out he glanced down at the front licence plate. It was a Belfast plate. They had thought of everything.

Together the two men walked back across the yard and got into a waiting motor car. Already the other men were preparing to leave with the empty lorry. "Best we get out ahead of them," McCann said, as he hurriedly turned the ignition key and drove the Riley through the gate and into the lane.

A short time later, the fog appeared to lift as the car accelerated and headed south along the coast road. "We'll hit the main road at Larne and from there it's a clear sail into Belfast. And right now the weather looks as if it's letting up at least for awhile; if it holds we should have no trouble at all getting you there in plenty of time to catch the Liverpool steamer."

In the back seat Meagher scarcely heard a word the other man said. His eyes were heavy with sleep. He yawned wearily, closed his eyes and allowed himself to drift into a deep sleep. And for just a moment, he was again aware of the sound of tires rolling on the wet pavement.

Chapter Eight

The two men hurriedly climbed into the army lorry parked a short distance from the house. Minutes later the lorry left the yard, reached the bottom of the lane and turned onto the secondary road that skirted the town of Cushendun. Just north of the town the road narrowed as it neared the coast. The weather, which had improved just a short time earlier, began to deteriorate rapidly as the wind from the sea carried a low bank of swirling fog and mist inland. The Belfast man sat behind the wheel seemingly indifferent to the weather outside. Beside him Jimmy Draper, the younger of the two, sat watching the road ahead and hoping that the driver would have the good sense to slow down. He was familiar with the road and knew how treacherous the narrow winding road could be, especially on a bad night, if a vehicle was travelling at excess speed. He knew too that less than a mile up the road it took a sharp ninety degree turn towards the sea. A short distance farther on, the road took another dangerous turn at a point where the surrounding countryside fell steeply into the sea. And still farther up the coast, close to where they planned to push the lorry into the sea, the land dropped even more steeply, almost vertically, into the Irish Sea. On the other side of the road the adjacent land hugged the slopes of Cushleake Mountain. On both sides a deep narrow ditch followed the road as it wound its way north before turning inland across the mountain towards the tiny village of Drumadoon.

For a time both men sat in silence, their gaze fixed on the pool of light thrown onto the road by the lorry's headlamps. The Belfast man cleared his throat and stuck the half smoked cigarette he was holding back into the corner of his mouth. "That Meagher is a piece of work I'll tell you. I never liked the bastard from the first time I laid eyes on him. Did you hear him....did you hear what he said when I asked about the Wicklow man? He's dead. That's all he said, shot by the RUC. Can you believe that? And did you hear the way he said it? That's what pissed me off the most," the Belfast man said, making no effort to conceal his contempt for a man he hated intensely. "It was as if it was none of our business and we had no right to ask him. Who the bloody hell does he think he is, would you tell me that?"

"I'm damned if I know, but I'll tell you one thing, it gives me the creeps to be in the same room with him... I don't like the bugger either and as far as I know, not many do."

"You're dead right about that. I don't think he gives a damn about anyone."

The lorry slowed as they rounded the first sharp turn in the road, then, just as quickly resumed its earlier pace. As they turned towards the sea the fog began to thicken and the lorry slowed almost to a crawl before finally coming to a stop in the middle of the road. It was then that the younger man decided it was time to say something. "Watch yourself as you come up to the next turn; it's a bad one and there's not so much as a hedge to prevent us from going off the road." For a moment, he stared nervously at the bank of fog lying across the road in front of the lorry. "It's not that long ago a car left the road, not far from here, and almost ended up in the sea. It can happen easily enough, especially in this kind of weather," he added, to drive the point home.

The other man nodded, but said nothing as the lorry began to move forward once again, this time at a more measured pace. For several minutes they sat watching the road ahead. It was the Belfast man who spoke first.

"Jimmy."

'What is it?"

"Och, I was just wondering if you still want out?"

"Aye...I'm thinking about it, now more than ever. It's my own fault, I know that, but I never thought it would come to this. Doing what we did before was one thing, but the killing is something else."

"For Christ sake Jimmy, sure the other crowd is doing the same thing. It's not as if we are the only ones doing it."

"Sure, I know that, but I want no bloody part of it. It's just not right."

"Jesus Jimmy, you should have thought about that before."

"Don't I know it."

"You know I won't say anything no matter what you do."

"Aye, I know that too."

"But, for God's sake Jimmy, be careful. You can image what will happen if Meagher ever got wind of this and there are others just like him. And I'll tell you something else. No one will lift a finger to help you if it comes to that, not even McCann, and he's better than most. And if you think about it, why would he, for like the rest of us he's convinced there's no other way for our people to get what they deserve. Remember that and make damn sure you know what you're doing before you do something you'll regret."

The lorry cautiously negotiated the second sharp bend in the road and headed north along the rugged coast road moving slowly at first and then at a more moderate speed as the fog lifted on the stretch of road immediately ahead of them. Without even being aware of it, Jimmy took his eyes off the road and thought about what the other man had just said. No one had to tell him it would probably end badly for him. That was something he had already figured out for himself. Like everyone else, he had heard rumours of how the IRA dealt with those who tried to leave. Some of the stories he conceded were probably exaggerated while others, he fearfully acknowledged, were probably true. Briefly he thought of his mother and father who knew nothing of his involvement with the IRA and he wondered what it would do to them if they ever found out.

He could not be certain, but now the lorry seemed to be moving faster than it had been a few minutes earlier. Instinctively he raised his head just in time to see the road ahead disappear in a blanket of heavy rain and fog. He felt the lorry shudder and lurch sideways as the Belfast man struggled to regain control. Suddenly he was thrown violently against the door and seconds later he felt the weight of the other man pressing down on him as the lorry rolled and left the road.

Chapter Nine

Thompson found his key and let himself in through the front door of the modest, but well kept two storey house in Nursery Avenue. The door was always kept closed in winter. The small front porch was dark, but he could see a light on in the kitchen at the end of the hall. He removed his wet coat and cap and hung them over the coat rack. Drying his face and the back of his neck with the damp cotton handkerchief he had used earlier in the evening, he stood for a moment before opening the door into the main hallway. There was a small coal fire burning in the darkened sitting room. Through the open door he could see its reflected light in the hall. Thompson walked across the carpeted room and stood in front of the fireplace. He rubbed his hands and held them over the fire. Thank God, for a bit of heat, he thought, as he moved closer to the hearth. Aside from the rain and the long walk home he had managed to spend another pleasant enough Saturday night having a quiet drink in familiar surroundings. Coleraine, like most towns in Ireland, had no shortage of public houses. Most were on this side of the river, some only a short distance from the house. The closest, on the corner of Chapel Square and Long Commons, was no more than a few minutes' walk from Nursery Avenue, but for whatever reason the place never appealed to him. Nor did the pubs that lined the one side of New Market Street. He was, like many of his generation, a creature of habit and preferred to take his drink across the Bann even if it meant a long trek on a winter's night.

"Is that you, Willie?" he heard his wife call from the kitchen.

"Aye... and who else would it be?"

"Well, that's the God's honest truth....nobody else in their right mind would be out on a night like this. You'd think at your age, you'd have enough sense to stay home when the weather's that bad.

"I suppose."

"I'm glad you're home, all the same. I was beginning to worry about you."

"Och, would you catch yourself on woman, sure what's there to worry about? It's not the first time I have come home half drenched, and sure it wasn't raining that hard when I left the house."

"Well, be that as it may, I was worried just the same. You're not getting any younger, you know, and one of these days you'll catch pneumonia the way you carry on." There was no anger in her voice, only concern. She was standing in the doorway wearing an apron covered in flour. "I'm doing a wee bit of baking," she added, wiping her hands on the apron. "You've probably forgotten, but last week after mass, I promised Mrs Sweeney I'd help out with the bake sale this year."

"As if you didn't have enough to do around here."

"Oh, I don't mind, I'm just happy to be able to help. You know how much I like to bake. I've had the house to myself so I'm almost finished. The last of the rolls are in the oven and almost ready. Maybe you'd like a wee roll with your tea?"

"Aye, I could stand a cup of tea and a bite to eat, right enough"

"Would you like me to help?"

"No, stay where you are and dry yourself off by the fire. I'll go and make you a bite of supper."

"You're a good woman, Mary."

"Och...!"

"No. I mean it.... to put up with the likes of me."

"Would you hold your tongue. You're a decent man Willie Thompson."

"I sometimes wonder."

"Ooh, don't be silly, of course, you are."

Mary could smell the whiskey on him from where she stood. He wasn't drunk, but his faced was flushed and he looked tired. His drinking had always bothered her. Not that he had ever been abusive, it was just that she had no tolerance for drink. She could never see the need of it. Still, she meant what she said. He was a decent man and she loved him dearly. And to be fair, he only drank on Saturday nights and never in the house, at least, not since the children were born. Other women were not so fortunate. Drink had wrecked many a home. He had been a good provider and had seen to it that they never went without, even when work was scarce. Perhaps she should try harder to be a little more understanding. The parish priest had said as much, during one of his visits. He had caught her at a bad time and she was sorry afterwards that she had mentioned it at all.

"I'll make your supper now," she said, as she turned and walked slowly back into the kitchen.

Thompson sat down in one of the comfortable chairs. He could hear the sound of the wind moaning in the chimney. A mild odour of coal soot hung about the room from the occasional draught forced down the chimney by a sudden gust of wind. It was an all too familiar smell. On an overcast day the air in the town often reeked of coal smoke. It was something you lived with and after awhile became so accustomed to that you paid it no heed. He unlaced his leather boots and set them by the fire to dry. His slippers were lying where he had left them the night before and within easy reach. Although still damp he was beginning to feel more comfortable now that he had settled himself directly in front of the warm fire. A short while later he heard his wife call him from the kitchen.

"I'm coming," he said, easing himself out of the chair.

The kitchen was warm from the hot oven and the lovely smell of freshly baked bread permeated the brightly lit room. The buttered rolls were steaming hot. A plate of sliced ham and cheese lay on the table in front of him. His wife had set some pickled onions out as well. He sat down at his usual spot at the end of the table and reached for a hot roll. Mary poured two cups of strong hot tea and sat down at the opposite end of the table. She had taken off her soiled apron and tidied her hair. She's still a good looking woman, he thought, as he reached across the table for a spoon to stir his tea.

"That's a lovely cup of tea."

Mary nodded in agreement, holding the hot cup between her hands.

"Are you not going to take a bite yourself?"

Mary shook her head. "No I don't think I'll bother, sure the tea will do me. My mother used to say, after you've cooked for everybody else, you're not that keen on eating yourself."

" I have heard you say that many a time."

Mary looked across the table at her husband. She was always pleased to see him eat something, especially after he'd been drinking. She knew from past experience he would feel the good of it in the morning and probably sleep better too.

"I was thinking we might drive over to Ballycastle in the morning."

"Aye, we could do that if you like."

She had learned over the years that he was agreeable to most things when he had been drinking. Drink seemed to have a mellowing effect on him. The youngsters had noticed it too and used it to good advantage on occasions. She remembered that was how they got their dog.

"We haven't seen Molly in over a month. It would be a nice surprise for her, don't you think? And now that wee Tommy's starting to walk maybe you'll be able to take him for a wee doddle on the street."

Thompson nodded. "I would enjoy that."

"Willie I know you'll not go yourself, but I'd like to go to mass in the morning. I thought we could leave right after, if that suited you."

"Aye, if that's what you want to do."

"You're sure you don't mind?"

Thompson shook his head, "no, why would I mind?"

She glanced at her husband and smiled. "Well, then, that's settled."

Thompson helped himself to another buttered roll and a slice of cooked ham. He felt more himself now. "I'll see what the weather's like in the morning and if it's not too cold we might take a wee run around the Causeway and perhaps drive down to the harbour at Dunseverick."

"Oh, that would be nice."

"We're going in that direction anyway and sure it's only a few miles out of our way and well worth an extra drop or two of petrol. And now that I think of it, it's been a while since we've been there."

"More tea Willie?"

"No."

"There's plenty in the pot."

"Och, no, I don't think I will."

"Are you sure, now?"

"Well... maybe just a wee drop."

Mary smiled, poured them both another cup of tea and put the empty teapot back on the cooker. She had noticed that as he grew older he wasn't always sure what he wanted. More often than not, he said no when he really meant yes. It was as if he had come to rely on her to help him make up his mind about ordinary things, things like a second cup of tea or an extra piece of toast. "There's a letter from Podraic you'll want to read. It seems he may be sent to a mission church in Africa after all, a place called Kagoro somewhere in Nigeria. I've never heard of it before, but apparently Irish Catholic missionaries have been there for a long time. He's to take the place of an Irish priest who died of yellow fever. I must say that part worries me...but the good news is he says he'll be at Dromantine in Newry for a short time before he goes and so we'll be able to see him before he leaves for Africa. Thanks be to God. For awhile I was worried we might not get the chance to see him at all for I'm sure it'll likely be awhile before we see him again. If you like I can read it to you while you finish your supper."

Thompson listened as his wife read aloud the contents of the letter from their eldest son. He would read it for himself, of course, but she always felt it best to make him aware of the important parts. It was her way of making sure he didn't miss anything. He was proud of all his children and Podraic as much as any of them. But unlike his son, he cared little for the dogma of the Catholic Church, or any other church, for that matter, including the Church of Ireland where he had been baptized and later confirmed by the Bishop of Connor. Mary had refused to marry him unless he became a Roman Catholic. Reluctantly, he had agreed, and the church saw to it that their children were raised in the Catholic faith. But he was a Catholic in name only. He rarely went to mass and when he did it was only out of consideration for the kind and gentle woman who sat at the other end of the table.

"Willie, are you listening?"

"I am...."

"I thought for a minute you were somewhere else."

"Well, if I was I had a speedy return."

Mary shook her head, annoyed that he didn't appear to be

paying as much attention as she felt he should. "He says he'll know for sure by Christmas."

"Aye well that's something, but does he say anything about coming home before then? It's been awhile since we've seen him."

"No....only that he's looking forward to seeing us when he can. God knows, I'd love to see him back home for good, but that's not to be I suppose."

"You wouldn't be a mother if you didn't."

"That's true."

"I miss him too, Mary. I may not say it as often as I should, but he's never far from my thoughts."

Mary neatly folded the letter and put it back in the envelope. She sat quietly for a moment reflecting on what he had just said.

"I've never doubted that for a minute, but I wish you'd write him and tell him that yourself. You know he thinks the world of you, and it would be so good for him to hear you say it. It's not the same when I say it for you. A father should be able to write to his own son and that's the God's honest truth."

Thompson nodded, "Aye... I know that."

"Well, then, why don't you just do it?"

Mary was right. She was always right about these kind of things especially when it came to the children. The trouble was he didn't seem to know where to begin. It wasn't for the want of trying, but the words never seemed to come and in the end he thought it best to leave well enough alone. It was a lot easier just to leave the letter writing to his wife for he knew she would always say the right thing. It was difficult for him to write a letter at the best of times. He was never really sure what he was supposed to say to his son, given his reluctance, even now, to accept the decision Podraic had taken. God knows he loved him, but as proud as he was of him, he had never been able to come to grips with his decision to become a priest. He was a gifted student and for a time had talked about becoming a solicitor.

103

When he told him of his decision to enter the priesthood he had not discouraged him, but it was a disappointment all the same for in his heart he had wanted something more for him. At the time he'd kept his true feelings to himself. He said nothing to anyone including his wife. As it turned out it was just as well for Podraic's mind was made up and so was his mother's.

"What age is he now?" Thompson asked, with some hesitation. For some reason or other he had trouble remembering the ages of the two boys.

"Dear God, do you not remember the age of your own son?" she said, shaking her head in disbelief. "Sure he's twenty eight on his next birthday."

"Boys o' boys, you'd hardly believe it."

"No...no you wouldn't."

"I don't know where the years have gone."

"I don't think any of us do."

"Mary, time's a funny thing isn't it. I mean when you're young you think it'll never end and then, as my uncle used to say, you go to bed one night and the next morning you wake up an oull man."

"I'm not sure I've heard you say that before, but there's some truth in it all the same."

"That's not to complain mind you."

"No. But you're right for it's not so long ago they were all running around the house. M' ma used to say when they're small you can gather them up the way a hen gathers her chicks and when you close the door at night you know where they all are. I used to think it would be nice to keep them that way."

"Darling, they're supposed to grow up."

"Ooh, I know, love, it's just that they seem to grow up so quickly and before you know it, they're gone from us."

"Hmm...."

"I sometimes think I could write my whole life on a page," she said, looking down at the worn wedding ring on her finger.

"Come on now, stop your fretting."

"No...I mean it."

"Sure they're all healthy and doing well for themselves. You know you wouldn't have it any other way."

"I know... we have been blessed." Her mood changed and she smiled as she reached across the table to touch her husband's hand. "We did have some grand times together, didn't we."

"Aye, indeed we did, and a few troubles along the way thrown in for good measure."

She nodded her head knowingly. "That too."

Thompson laughed. "Mary, do you remember the night our Bertie and a wee fellow from across the river, I've forgotten his name now....anyway, the two of them dug up the front lawn of the Church of Ireland Rectory on the Mountsandel Road."

"How could I ever forget it?"

"The canon told me that when he woke up the next morning and looked out the bedroom window he saw the letters IRA cut out on the lawn. I'm laughing now, but at the time it was no laughing matter. I remember offering to pay to have someone repair the damage, but he would have none of it, and insisted instead that the two boys make restitution by doing the work themselves. He told the police the same thing. And right enough, that's what they did and it taught them a good lesson."

"I don't think I've ever been so humiliated in my whole life. I remember you weren't in the house when the policeman arrived at our front door with half the street looking on. He was a terrible wee fellow when he was growing up. For awhile he never seemed to be out of bother of one kind or another. Thank God it was never that serious although I suppose it was serious enough at the time. Mind you, having said that, it was the one and only time the police ever came to our door."

"Aye, they were never back. And to look at him now sure you'd hardly believe it was the same wee boy."

"Well, you know what they say....the apple doesn't fall far

from the tree. He's a lot like his father."

"I suppose he is, but sure didn't he turn out alright".

"He did and so did you."

"Aye, I suppose I did, but my own father didn't live long enough to see that. I think it would have set his mind at ease. God knows I must have been an awful worry to him. Even now, I find it hard to fathom how I managed to get myself into so much trouble when I had a father that cared as much as he did. He deserved better. It wasn't that he didn't try to warn me often enough about running with the wrong crowd. But one thing leads to another and before you know what's happened it's no longer innocent fun and the police are banging on the door. I think that's my biggest regret. I wish he had lived long enough to see that I didn't turn out so badly after all, in spite of all the trouble I caused him."

"Maybe he knew all along you'd be alright in the end."

"Perhaps he did. I'd like to believe that. All the same it would have been nice if he'd seen it for himself."

"Now, who's fretting?"

"Oh I don't mean to. It's just that for a time he was the most important person in my life. I learned so much from him, stuff that I remember to this day. The sad thing is, I felt I let him down in other ways too. I mean in school, before I got into all the trouble. I wasn't much of a student you know, and I think that bothered him more than he let on. It wasn't that I didn't try. It was just that I found it hard to keep up with the rest of the class. I remember my teacher at the Irish Society School going around the room a few days before the end of the school term assessing the performance of each student and when he came to me he smiled and shook his head and said he didn't think I would be able to pass the final exam. There was only one other boy in the class whose ability was called into question, but in his case the teacher held out the faint hope that he might just squeak through. I remember smiling awkwardly, trying to save face in front of the rest of the class....doing the best I could I suppose to hide the hurt and embarrassment I felt inside. But what I remember most to this day was the way he said it. It was said in kindness for I think it troubled him deeply that he was unable to offer more encouragement. A few days later I recall asking one of the smarter boys in the class if he would help me. He said he would, but when I rode my bike to Portstewart on the following Sunday afternoon he wasn't really interested."

There was a long silence before Mary spoke. He had never told her this before and it hurt her to hear the pain in his voice over something that had happened so long ago. "Well, love, you've done better than most in spite of it all."

Thompson hesitated for a moment. "I suppose I have, but it's the sort of thing a person never really forgets. When I failed the exam my father said it was because I was from a working class family. He didn't think it was right that I was required to fill in my father's occupation on the exam paper. I know he was disappointed, but he never stopped believing in me and I think he said what he did so that I wouldn't blame myself or feel any less of myself. And do you know, failing that exam bothered me for a long time and what made it worse, there was no second chance. I would have liked to have gone on in school and made something of myself. I have always thought that if things had turned out differently it would have pleased him. What he wanted most was for his children to have a better chance than he'd had for himself."

She reached across the table and gently squeezed his hand. "You would have liked him, Mary. My father was a good man."

"Darling, I'm sure of it."

After a few moments of silence, she rose from the table and started to gather up the dishes. Only a few slices of cooked ham remained on the plate. She was pleased that he had taken a good supper. It was nice to have him home just to sit for a while around the kitchen table and talk. She picked up the ham and carried it into the pantry. When she returned she sat down at the table facing her husband.

"Willie, there's something I've been meaning to say to you."

"What is it?"

"You won't be upset, will you?"

"I won't know until you tell me, will I now?"

"No, I don't suppose you will."

"Well, then."

"Oh, it's just that I wish you'd think about coming to mass more often. It might do you the world of good."

"Sure, we've been through all of that before."

"I know we have. It's just that it doesn't seem right somehow."

Thompson shook his head. "Mary, would you give your head peace, for both our sakes."

"Darling, I know we've talked about it before, but we never seem to get anywhere."

"Then, why would you bother?"

"Oh, it's just that I think you should go somewhere. And God help me, I never thought I'd hear myself say it, but if you'd be more at ease in the Church of Ireland why don't you go there? You always said how much nicer St. Patrick's was. Mind you, I won't go with you, but maybe you could go once in a while by yourself."

"Well, that's a new spin on things, I'll grant you that."

"It's just that I'd rather see you going to the Church of Ireland than nowhere at all."

"That doesn't say much for the Church of Ireland, does it?"

"Oh, you know what I mean..."

"Well, remind me to tell the new canon that the next time I see him down the town."

"I might as well talk to the dog for all the satisfaction I get out of you."

"Aye, well, now that you mention it maybe the dog will go

with me to St. Patrick's. I doubt that he'll set foot in the chapel. I hate to be the one to break it to you but I think that wee dog of ours is a Protestant. Sure he'll eat anything on a Friday."

"Oh, go on with yourself. I can see I'm wasting my breath. Mind you, it wouldn't be the first time and I doubt it'll be the last," she said, shaking her head and rising hurriedly from the table before she said something she might later regret. She wouldn't dare tell him, but she had asked Podraic and the parish priest to pray for him. She had to admit, however, that her efforts had not been blessed with much success and she was beginning to wonder if she was asking too much of the Blessed Virgin. It might be easier to pray for his return to the Church of Ireland. She put on her apron and started to pile the dishes in the sink.

"Willie...you're not annoyed with me, are you?"

"And if I was, do you think it would make any difference?"

"I meant no harm...you know that."

"Aye, well, I'll take your word for it."

"It's just that...."

"There's no need to say anymore."

"No I don't suppose there is, but you will think about it...."

"Mary, will you let it go?"

"Alright, I will, I promise," she said, not altogether convincingly. "Now go on into the other room and sit down by the fire. I won't be long cleaning up in here."

"Will you come in yourself?"

"Aye...we'll see."

In the sitting room the fire was beginning to wane, but the room was still warm. He poked the fire back to life and added a few lumps of coal. Within minutes the fire was blazing away again. Thompson settled into the same chair he had vacated a short time earlier and stretched his legs out in front of the fireplace to help dry the bottom of his trousers which were still damp to the touch. The earlier effects of the whiskey were beginning to wear off. The long walk home and the bite to eat had helped clear his head. He enjoyed drinking, but lately he had noticed a change in his tolerance for alcohol. Now he was satisfied to have two or three glasses of whiskey over the course of the evening. He lit a cigarette and sat quietly watching the fire. Bobbie Corbett was right, he had a lot to be thankful for. Mary was a devoted wife and a wonderful mother to their children. He couldn't have wished for anyone better had he planned it himself and he wondered how it was he had been so fortunate. Her whole life revolved around her family and her church. His father had often told him there was nothing more important than a man's family. Families look after one another and willingly bear one another's burdens. That's what he remembered his father saying and he in turn had told his own children the same thing. Mary was the glue that held the family together.

"Did you say something?" he heard his wife call from the kitchen.

"No.... no, I didn't."

"Were you talking to yourself again?"

"I don't think so."

"I'll be there in a minute. I'm just going upstairs to turn on the electric heater in the bedroom."

"Sure I could've done that."

"Oh, I don't mind, stay where you are."

Content to sit where he was he made no effort to get up. Besides, Mary was already half way up the stairs. He thought of his father again who for one reason or another had been on his mind most of the evening. He could see the black horses pulling the hearse down Long Commons. A small crowd of people had gathered on the street outside Saint Patrick's Church and as the procession moved along Church Street towards the Diamond, some of the men fell in behind and walked to the cemetery on the Portrush Road. As was the custom, his father had been laid out in the front room overlooking the street and the night before his mother had made up a bed on the couch and stayed with him all night. At first he refused to go in to see him telling his mother he wanted to remember his father the way he was. But when she insisted he should go into the room and see his own father before they carried him out of the house he reluctantly did what she had asked. He remembered too that at the cemetery he told his mother he didn't want to stay to see his father lowered into the ground, but she said he had to be there for it wasn't right to leave the burial of a loved one to strangers. And so with his younger brother he stood quietly by her side and together they each threw a handful of dirt on top of the coffin as it was lowered into the ground. And afterwards, when everyone else had left, he watched his mother kneel by the grave in silence. Your father got a great send off today. It's what he would have wanted, she told them after they returned to the empty house. Later, when his younger brother had fallen asleep he heard her crying upstairs in her room. He wanted to comfort her, to tell her it would be alright, but he knew in his heart it would not. And so he sat alone quietly sobbing in the front room until it was dark, all the while, waiting for his mother to come downstairs, but she never came and he fell asleep on the couch in his new suit.

The next day he went to settle up with Mr McFadden, the undertaker, and when he asked how much the family owed, the old man said two pounds, if you have it, son, and if you don't, I'll get it off the people up the Lodge Road. They can afford it. He had the two pound, but he never forgot the old man's expression of kindness and his willingness to help a family in need. Some people were like that in those days he remembered, it was their way of helping a working class family get by when they needed help the most. And God knows some of them needed all the help they could get, he thought, as he butted his cigarette and placed the small china ashtray back on the hearth. His wet clothes were almost dry, only the back of his collar and the cuffs of his trousers felt slightly damp. He had already thrown his overcoat and cap over the hot water tank before sitting down to his supper. They would be dry by morning.

"There, that's done. By the time we go bed the room should be as warm as toast," Mary said, easing herself into the other large comfortable chair in front of the fire.

"What...what's that you say?" he said, suddenly aware of her presence.

"Did I startle you?"

"No... I think I must have dozed off for a moment, that's all."

"You know, I've always liked this room," she said, rubbing her hands gently with hand lotion.

"You never had much time to enjoy it, what with looking after the house and raising the children."

"Oh, it wasn't so bad, I'd gladly do it over again," she replied, smiling as she lay back in the chair.

"Mary, have you heard anything more from the doctor?"

"No, not yet. He thought it might be a few weeks before we hear from the Royal."

"Has he said anything?"

"No... nothing, other than what he has already told me. I don't think he's too concerned to tell you the truth. He just thought it wise to have me seen by one of the specialist in Belfast. He seems to have a lot of faith in the doctors at the Royal."

"Aye, and well he should, you'll not find a better hospital anywhere."

"Well, Doctor Maclean certainly thinks so."

"Well, there you are."

Mary nodded. "When I hear from them I was thinking we might take the train and make a day of it" she said cheerfully, in an effort to avoid further questions. What she hadn't yet told him was that the doctor had said she might need to have an operation if her condition got any worse. For now she would keep that to herself. There didn't seem to be any point in worrying the family until she had something more definite to tell them. She would know soon enough and when she did that would be time enough to tell them.

"It would be nice to take the train."

"Well, then, that's something else to look forward to," she said, with enthusiasm. "And if you don't mind, we could walk over to Smithfield's and have a look at the shops; it's handy enough to York Street Station and afterwards we could have a late lunch before heading back to catch the afternoon train."

"Aye, we could do that easy enough. We haven't been in Belfast for some time so we might as well make the most of it."

"It has been awhile."

"Mary."

"What is it, love."

"You're sure you've told me everything."

"Of course I have... there's nothing to worry about, you'll see."

"You know I'm daft about you, don't you."

"Yes...I know," she said, reaching for his hand and gently holding it in her own. "I'm a very lucky woman."

They sat in silence. Neither of them, it seemed, had anything further they needed or wanted to say. It was enough just to sit together in a warm familiar room and watch the fire flickering in the hearth.

Closing his eyes he drifted into sleep, content to let his mind wander where it pleased. He saw the early morning sun bathe the room in shafts of dazzling light. And just inside the door, near the front of the auditorium, a small boy stood in the company of other boys who had gathered with their teachers for morning assembly. The headmaster, an old man with thinning grey hair and a kind wrinkled face, looked about the room and waited for the noise to subside. The old man motioned with his hand, and in unison they raised their voices in joyful song:

Summer suns are glowing over land and sea;
Heavenly breezes flowing, bountiful and free;

Everything rejoices in the mellow rays;
Earth's ten thousand voices swell the psalm of praise.

Chapter Ten

Father Nolan had not slept well in the chair. He wasn't sure of the exact time, but it was sometime after midnight when he awoke to the sound of the grandfather clock chiming in the hall. He managed to get to his feet and climb the staircase to his own bed. It was a manoeuvre he was well accustomed to and presented no more than the usual hazards associated with an old man climbing the stairs in the middle of the night. He had even managed to find the bottom of his pyjamas and pull them on before falling asleep on the top of the bed. An hour later, half awake, he dragged himself under the covers and went back to sleep. Occasionally, the effort was beyond him and he went to bed either fully dressed or half naked. Mrs Cassidy, in an effort to improve his odds, had started laying his pyjamas out on top of the bed before she left for the evening. The arrangement appeared to be working although she had no way of knowing for sure.

There was no fireplace in the bedroom and in winter it was bitterly cold early in the morning. Shivering against the cold he threw first one leg and then the other over the edge of bed. He braced himself as his feet touched the cold hardwood floor. At that hour of the morning the bed was the only warm place in the house and he was sorely tempted to crawl back under the heavy eiderdown and go back to sleep. He stretched out his arms and slowly rose to his feet steadying himself against the bed to maintain his balance. He stood for a moment to catch his breath before reaching for his slippers and pulling on his dressing gown. Satisfied that he could remain upright, he crossed the room into the hallway and made his way to the bathroom on the other side of the house. Stooping down he switched on the small electric heater and closed the bathroom door behind him. He didn't feel well and had no reason to believe he would feel any better as the day wore on. Over the years it was something he'd learned to live with for the piper he knew always had to be paid. Mind you, he thought as he timidly held his forehead, the piper seems bent on extracting more than his fair share this morning.

For as long as he could remember, it was his habit to rise early on a Sunday morning regardless of how late he went to bed the night before or how much he had to drink. Rising early after a night of heavy drinking he had come to regard as a kind of penance. But there was more to it than that. Rising early on a Sunday morning not only gave him time to clear his head, but more importantly, it gave him the time he needed to prepare himself mentally and spiritually for the celebration of mass. In his heart he believed God was faithful and that the salvation of the small flock entrusted to his dubious care would not be frustrated by the intemperance of a foolish old man. He would perform his priestly functions well enough, few would be any the wiser, and God he was certain would do the rest.

The room was warmer now as Father Nolan turned off the hot water tap and cautiously lowered himself into the large ornate bath that stood on four elaborate iron feet. He laid his head back and closed his eyes, content now to let the hot water soothe his weary old limbs. The homily, which had been prepared earlier in the week seemed to be lacking something and as he lay in the warm bath turning it over in his mind it occurred to him that maybe a few things needed to be added. The more he thought about it the more convinced he became that something was missing and it troubled him that he hadn't been able to put his finger on it.

Father Nolan was an eloquent speaker with a flair for the dramatic that on occasion startled the more elderly members of the congregation, especially those who had unwittingly dropped off during the sermon. During his long career, more than one Bishop had commented on his exceptional gift. One in particular he remembered, a somewhat disagreeable man from County Mayo, had gone so far as to suggest he'd missed his calling. A pity he had said, for had he chosen to pursue a career on the stage he might have enjoyed some notoriety at the Abbey. He paid the man little heed for sure he knew full well Bishops were notorious liars.

After much deliberation he had chosen to speak on the deity of Christ. He had taken for his text a passage from Saint Paul's letter to the small band of Christians at Colossae where the apostle urges them to reject the false teaching of those who would question the divinity of Christ declaring him to be something other than the son of the one true and living God. Lying in the comfort of the warm bath he reflected upon the words of the great apostle and his unwavering commitment to the risen Christ. As he did so he came to the realization that the homily was as much for him as for anyone else. Had he not himself in moments of unspoken doubt questioned the divine nature of the Christ he had vowed to serve? He closed his eyes and sought forgiveness. In that moment of contrition he knew again what he had always known, that it was God who was at work within him giving him the will and the power to achieve his purpose.

A few minutes later he reluctantly eased himself out of the bath and slowly dried himself off with one of the large towels Mrs Cassidy had laid out the night before. The old priest wrapped the towel around his belly and walked back to the bedroom. After the hot bath, the room now felt even colder than it had been when he first climbed out of bed. Mrs Cassidy was supposed to have made arrangements with her son the electrician to have a heater installed in the bedroom, but if her past performance was anything to go by, he was unlikely to see the heater anytime soon. He dressed as quickly as he could and cautiously descended the stairs into the drawing room. On Sundays Mrs Cassidy arrived late in the afternoon just in time to prepare the evening meal. She had reminded him sharply, on more than one occasion, that it was his job to light the fire on Sunday morning and to look after himself as best he could until she arrived later in the day. He opened the damper and struck a match. Immediately the dry kindling caught and within minutes the fire was crackling loudly in the fireplace. "There. By the time I get back the house will be warmer," he muttered, as he turned and walked across the room to the chair he had left the night before. The empty whiskey bottle lay on the floor where it had fallen. He would have to get rid of it before she arrived to prepare the evening meal and it would be wise to do it now in case he might forget to do it later. There's no future in giving her cause to speak her mind the minute she walks through the door for God knows it doesn't take much to set that woman off, he thought, as he picked up the empty whiskey bottle and carried it into the kitchen.

Father Nolan held the crucifix hanging about his neck, closed his eyes and raising it to his lips gently kissed the crucified Christ. He placed the open missal on the small table beside his chair, covered his face with his hands, and kneeling bowed in earnest prayer.

Christ be with me, Christ within me,

Christ behind me, Christ before me,
Christ beside me. Christ to win me,
Christ to comfort and restore me....

In the silence of the empty room he sought once more to enter into the presence of his God. It was a sacred moment; a time of wonder and renewal. A time when he opened his heart and mind to the spirit of the living God who dwelt within him, to the one whom God the Father had lifted up and given a name above all names. Again he sought forgiveness for his many failures and devoutly prayed, as he had done so often in the past, that God would grant him a faithful heart. He prayed too that when he rose to feed the flock of Christ with the word and the blessed sacrament God would be glorified. In an act of priestly contrition he would bow down before the altar and declare himself unworthy.

Down in adoration falling,
Lo! the sacred host we hail;
Lo! o'er ancient forms departing
Newer rites of grace prevail;
Faith for all defects supplying
Where the feeble senses fail.

Slowly, he rose to his feet and stood for a few moments in silence before making his way into the front hallway. The old priest pulled on his overcoat, wrapped a woollen scarf around his neck and stepped outside into the bright cold morning that heralded a new day.

A few of the older members of the parish were already beginning to arrive for mass as he crossed the lawn and entered the chapel through the side door.

"Father, there's a big man in there wants to have a word with you."

"Who is it Sean?" Father Nolan said, removing his overcoat and turning to face a small red haired altar boy who stood pointing excitedly at the door behind him.

"I don't know Father, he's not from around here."

"Well, what does he want?"

"I don't know that either... but he says he needs to speak to you."

"Does he, now."

"Aye, and I don't much care for the look of him either, Father."

"Och, would you howl' your tongue."

"He's got shifty eyes."

"Never mind that nonsense. What did you tell him?"

"I told him you weren't here yet, sure what else would I tell him? I didn't tell him to bugger off, if that's what you're thinking."

The old priest shook his head. "I'll have none of that out of you...you should be ashamed of yourself talking like that and you an altar boy. I've a good mind to speak to your mother."

The boy shrugged his shoulders. "For what? Sure my da uses that word all the time, bugger this and bugger that, he says."

"God help me, you're incorrigible," the old priest said, controlling his anger. A good cuff on the ear or a mouthful of soap might do him the world of good, he thought, but that he knew was a matter for his parents to deal with. Not that it was likely to do any good for they'd shown little inclination to set any kind of example for the boy. The mother meant well enough but she seemed incapable of doing anything with him and the father, who was a bit of a drifter, didn't seem to care much one way or the other what the boy did.

The boy didn't know what the word meant, but he was not about to ask for an explanation. If the look on the old man's face was anything to go by, he'd just as soon not know.

"Where is he now?"

"Sure, didn't I just tell you... he's in there...in the chapel."

"You're a cheeky wee fellow, too."

"Not as cheeky as your man. Sure didn't he just walk in here a minute ago, as brazen as a brass monkey, walked right passed the altar and never so much as lowered his head... he's not one of us, Father, I'm sure of that."

"Didn't I just tell you to howl' your tongue?"

"You did, Father."

"I'll have no more of that, then....."

"Speak of the devil Father, there he is."

"Father Nolan?"

"Aye, the same."

"Sir, I wonder if I might have a few words with you in private."

"And who might you be?" the priest said, annoyed at the sudden and untimely appearance of a man he had never seen before.

"Forgive me, sir, the name's Hamill...Inspector James Hamill of the RUC," the policeman said, holding out his hand. "I was told I might find you here. I hope it's not inconvenient."

"I'm afraid it is, Inspector....I can spare you very little time just now. I'm about to celebrate mass."

"I'm sorry, sir."

"You're not a Catholic, then."

"No sir, I am not."

"You have the look of a Baptist about you," Father Nolan said, regaining his composure.

"No, actually, I'm a Presbyterian, sir."

"Who would have thought it," the old priest said, mildly amused at the other man's apparent discomfort. "You're sure...."

"Quite sure, sir."

"Well, then, I don't suppose there's any point in inviting you to stay for Sunday Mass."

"No, Father, but thank you just the same."

"I haven't much time Inspector, a few minutes at the most."

121

"Yes, I gathered that sir."

"Sean, away with you, like a good wee fellow. I'll catch up with you in a minute." He waved the boy out the door with the back of his hand. "And pull the door shut after you."

Father Nolan waited until he was gone. "Now Inspector, what is it you wanted to see me about?"

"Sir, you may not have heard, but there was a bombing in Ballycastle last night."

"God help us, you don't say, were there casualties?"

"I'm afraid so; three people are dead including two police officers."

"In Ballycastle of all places, I would never have believed it."

"There's more, sir. Early this morning, quite by accident really, we found an Army lorry that had overturned and burned on the coast road near Runabay Head, not far from here. We think you might be able to help us."

"Good God, man.... how?"

Chapter Eleven

He thought he heard his wife call from the foot of the stairs that his breakfast was on the table. When she called the second time he was quite certain and quickly finished dressing.

"I'll be right down."

Glancing in the dresser mirror he knotted a dark red and grey paisley tie. There, that'll do rightly, he thought, as he tucked his shirt into his trousers and slipped the suspenders over his shoulders.

"Willie, did you hear me?"

"Aye, I'm coming."

"I want you to have it while it's nice and hot."

"I'll be right there."

He hurried down the stairs into the warm kitchen. Mary was wearing a dark blue tailored suit and a white silk blouse. She looked very smart. He couldn't remember seeing it on her, but thought better of asking if it was new in case it was something she'd worn before and he hadn't noticed. He had made that mistake in the past and wasn't about to make it again anytime soon. The dark colour suits her, he thought, as he sat down at the table and reached for the bottle of HP sauce.

"I've fried you up a wee bit of black pudding as a special treat this morning. I know how much you like it. Mind you, I don't think it's as nice as we normally buy."

"Oh, I'm sure it'll be alright."

"Well, I hope you enjoy it.

Thompson was hungry. He had enjoyed a decent night's sleep and was ready for a good meal. With the exception of the black pudding, his wife had cooked his usual Sunday morning breakfast, bacon and eggs, a pork sausage and two small pieces of fried potato bread. For the past year he had been having a little stomach trouble and the doctor had suggested he cut down on fried foods and limit himself to one or two fries a week. Mary had seen to it that he did what the doctor ordered and now had him down to one fry a week. The ends of one of the sausages had burst open and the minced pork was fried to a lovely deep brown colour. They were nice and crisp too. Since he was a boy, he had always eaten the end pieces first; it was the best part of the sausage. His father he remembered had done the same thing. He cut off the biggest end, dipped it in the HP sauce and put it in his mouth. "Boys, you can't beat the Pork Shop when it comes to a pork sausage," he said, smiling.

"No, they're hard to beat."

"Are you not going to have one yourself? Here why don't you have a wee piece of mine."

Mary shook her head, she much preferred a slice of toast and marmalade. Only occasionally did she fancy a sausage and a few strips of bacon. This morning she was content to have her buttered toast and marmalade.

"More tea?"

"Aye."

Thompson was fond of his tea. He held his cup out as she poured him another large cup.

"You're looking very smart."

"Ooh, go on with you."

"No. I mean it. Sure you look lovely."

"Well, it's nice of you to say so. Go on now finish your breakfast, I've seen that look before."

"If you weren't off out the door, I'd suggest we...."

"Oh hush! behave yourself." She caught his eye and smiled. "Not that I'd mind." she added, almost in a whisper.

"Well, then."

"Oh, would you stop now, and Aggie in the house too."

"Come on over here...."

"I'll do no such thing. Look at the time," she said, pressing a finger to his lips. "You'll just have to wait."

"I suppose I will."

She stooped down and kissed him lightly on the forehead. "There, be good."

Before she had a chance to retreat he put his arms around her waist and pulled her gently to him.

"I really have to be off now, darling."

Thompson nodded and released her.

"I'll walk back from mass if it's all the same to you. It looks like a lovely morning after all and I think I would enjoy the walk. A bit on the cool side mind you, but that's to be expected this time of the year. It'll do me the world of good."

"You'll do no such thing, I'll pick you up in the car. Sure, we can just as easily go on from there."

"No, it would be better if I came back to the house first. I've a few things I need to do before I go. Besides I really feel like walking this morning."

"Suit yourself."

"I'll walk straight home from the chapel, then. That way you'll have more time to finish your breakfast before you have to get the car. I know you don't like to be rushed on a Sunday morning."

"I'll fetch the car and wait for you here," he said, willing now to let the matter rest for it was clear she had made up her mind.

"That'll be grand, and don't forget now there's more tea in the teapot."

She left the kitchen and went into the hall to collect her hat and coat. A few moments later Thompson heard the front door close behind her. It's just as well, he thought; it'll take a good twenty minutes to get the car and drive it back.

He returned to his breakfast in earnest. The eggs were cooked just the way he liked them, not runny, but not hard either. The bacon too was just right. He reached for the HP sauce. It was a new bottle, and again he had to shake it several times to get the thick dark sauce through the narrow neck. It was worth the effort for eggs always tasted better with a bit of HP. The potato bread which had a wonderful taste on its own he preferred to eat plain or dipped in egg yolk. He poured himself another cup of tea and sat back down content to enjoy the rest of his breakfast at a leisurely pace.

When he had finished he carried the dirty dishes to the sink. Out of habit he turned on the wireless and stood over the sink looking beyond the kitchen window into the sheltered backyard surrounded on three sides by a tall cedar hedge. The hedge would have to be trimmed and the lawn cut before it got much colder, he reminded himself again. He had intended to do it earlier in the week, but for whatever reason he just hadn't got around to it. Trimming the hedge was a big job and it was beginning to dawn on him that, at his age, it might be wise to think about paying someone to do the work for him. Mary had suggested the same thing and had even found a person who was prepared to do the work for a reasonable price. It made her nervous she said to see him up the ladder reaching across the top of the hedge with the clippers while trying to balance on the ladder. He started to wash the dishes and stack them on the drying rack beside the sink, not paying particular attention to the

BBC announcer hosting the Sunday morning broadcast from London. Then he heard it.

We interrupt this program to bring you a special bulletin from Northern Ireland. A powerful explosion rocked the town of Ballycastle late last night killing two police officers and an unidentified British soldier. At least two other persons are known to be injured....

"Oh dear God!" A saucer slipped from his hand and fell back into the sink. Shocked by what he had just heard he walked across the room and turned up the volume.

The Home Secretary, Sir Nigel Hathaway, has condemned the bombing as a cowardly and brutal act of terrorism....

"God help us," he shouted angrily.

Like many others in the six counties he had grown accustomed, in recent months, to hearing reports of trouble in places like Derry and Belfast, but it was something you didn't expect to hear happening in a peaceful town like Ballycastle. It would be like bombing Coleraine, he thought, and who in their right mind would believe a thing like that?

Drying the last of the silverware he reached over and turned off the wireless. "You'd think, in this day and age, there'd be a better way to settle their differences. But that doesn't seem very likely, and God help us, the one crowd's as bad as the other," he said, hurriedly folding the dishcloth and hanging it over the back of the chair.

Shaken, he left the kitchen and went back upstairs to finish dressing. He reached for his dark blazer, but changed his mind and instead put on the new Harris Tweed jacket his wife had bought for him a few months earlier. It'll go better with the paisley tie, he thought. Over the past few months he had gained a few pounds around his waist, not much, but just enough to leave a small crease in the jacket when the centre button was done up. Straightening himself up he glanced at his image in the mirror. There, sure it was hardly noticeable, and besides, hadn't he just eaten a big breakfast.

Pulling the front door shut behind him, he set off down the street to pick up the car he kept in a rented garage close to the park. A garage was hard to come by in the town and he considered himself lucky to have found one within reasonable walking distance from the house. Since buying the new car he had made a habit of filling her with petrol before putting her away. That way she was always ready for the road.

The weather had cleared, at least in Coleraine, and to the northeast the sky also looked promising. It might turn out to be a good day for a drive, after all, he thought, as he turned the corner into Nursery Avenue and parked the Morris sedan in front of the house. Mary wasn't back yet, but he expected her anytime now. He threw his overcoat over one of the chairs and sat down in the sitting room to wait. Upstairs, he could hear their youngest daughter running the bath water. She hadn't gone to mass and her mother wasn't too pleased. Earlier in the morning, he'd heard a brief, but heated exchange between them. Aggie was a good girl all the same, and had given them no bother worth mentioning. Thompson was fond of her and tended to take her part when she found herself at odds with her mother, although this morning he'd had the good sense to stay out of it. He lit a cigarette, picked up the small china ashtray he had used the night before and placed it on the arm of the chair. As a rule, he didn't smoke in the car and it would be awhile before he would have a chance to enjoy another one. That was the one concession he made to his wife and for the most part he'd kept his word.

"Good morning, Daddy."

"Well, well.... I thought you were taking a bath."

"I was... I mean... I am. I'm just running the water."

She poured herself a small glass of orange juice and came back into the room. "Oh dear, I don't think I'm wide awake yet," she said, in a sleepy voice. "I don't think I slept very well."

"I'm not surprised."

"Oh, daddy, not you too."

"No, but you look tired, Aggie."

"I am," she said, struggling to hold back another yawn.

"Did you enjoy the dance?"

"I did... but I really should've come home earlier."

"I think your mother would agree with you."

"I know she would. She has already told me as much. She's not back yet is she?"

"No, but I'm expecting her any minute. We're going to drive over to Ballycastle to see Molly."

"That will be lovely."

"Would you like to come?"

"Oh, I would, I would love to daddy, but I think I'd better stay home and catch up on my lessons."

"You're sure."

"Yes, quite."

"Well, I'll tell Molly you were asking for her."

"Oh, please do."

She left the room and went back upstairs to have her bath. It might be just as well to be in the bath when her mother came home, she thought, closing the bathroom door behind her and quietly turning the lock.

A few minutes later Thompson heard the front door open and his wife call from the hallway.

"Darling, I'm home.

"I'm in here."

She poked her head in through the door. "I won't be more than a few minutes, honestly."

"Would you like me to put the kettle on before we go?"

"No, not unless you're having a cup yourself."

"No... I don't think I will."

"You're sure... you won't get a cup until we get to Molly's.

"No, I'll wait"

"Is Aggie up?"

"She is, but she is not coming with us."

"I should think not. If she's not well enough to go to mass, she's not well enough to go touring all over the countryside in a motor car... and I hope you told her that..."

"Mary, would you give your head peace."

"I will not."

"Have you forgotten what it was like to be her age?"

"When I was her age I went to mass."

"Oh, I don't doubt that for a minute," he said, annoyed at her persistence. He butted his cigarette and grabbed his overcoat. "I'll be waiting in the car," he shouted after her as she headed up the stairs.

"Aye, well, please yourself."

Thompson started the car and waited.

Within minutes she appeared at the front door. "There, that's done," she said, settling herself down on the seat beside him.

"We're off then."

"We are...."

"You're not still upset are you?" Thompson asked, as the car pulled away from the curb.

"No... I'm over it."

"There's been a bombing in Ballycastle. It was on the news this morning while you were at chapel."

"When...?"

"Sometime last night, they said."

"Dear Mother of God.... was anyone hurt?"

"Aye, I'm afraid so... and at least three dead"

"Ooh, dear God."

"A soldier, and two police officers."

"Oh, Willie, that's terrible," she said, visibly upset by what he

130

had just told her. "I hope and pray it's nobody Molly knows. What kind of people would do a thing like that?"

Thompson shook his head. "I honestly don't know."

"Nor do I, but I'm glad we decided to go to Ballycastle after all. Molly's bound to be upset and she'll be all the more pleased to see us, I'm sure."

"Aye..."

Thompson made his way through the town and out the Bushmills road. The weather, he knew, could change quickly along the coast, especially in winter.

"Mary."

"What is it, darling?"

"You don't mind if we take a wee run down to the harbour as planned. It's only a few miles out of our way. We'll see what the weather's like on the coast, of course. I thought we might just sit in the car for a few minutes, once we get there."

"No, I don't mind. I don't suppose a few minutes will make much difference, one way or the other."

"Are you warm enough?"

"Oh, aye, I'm just lovely."

Thompson turned and smiled. "You are indeed."

She pretended not to hear him, but she was pleased all the same. He always noticed her and it was nice to know that after all this time he still made a fuss over how smart she looked.

For the next several miles they drove on in silence, content to watch the countryside drifting past. At Bushmills they crossed the stone bridge over the river and turned left onto the main street that ran through the centre of the town. The car passed the war memorial and moments later a row of thatched cottages, before starting up the long steep hill towards the Fingers. On either side of the road, aged, moss covered trees reached out in a tangled embrace, forming a dark canopy high above the road. At the top of the hill the road forked and Thompson turned towards the Giant's Causeway. A short time later he pulled the car over to the side of the road and together they climbed a grassy embankment on the opposite side of the road. The view of the Antrim and Derry coastline was magnificent. From their vantage point high above the road they could see the town of Portrush and nearby the Skerries, lying like a great whale in a sparkling sea. In the distance, Downhill and the hills of Donegal were visible in the clear morning air.

It was as he remembered it.

"Boys o' boys there's a grand sight."

Mary nodded. "It's lovely, right enough."

"We'll go on to the harbour, then?"

"Yes, let's," she said excitedly, taken up by her husband's enthusiasm.

He eased the car back onto the road and drove the short distance to the Giant's Causeway. Opposite the Causeway gate the car slowed almost to a stop as it reached the top of the hill and turned sharply to follow the coast road that would take them to the habour

Within minutes they reached the ancient ruins of Dunseverick Castle and started down towards the small village that guarded the narrow road leading to the harbour. Thompson touched the brake and the car slowed. "Look! there's Rathlin Island, you can almost make out the shape of the lighthouse at Bull Point. Can you see it Mary? There, at this end of the island," he said, pointing off in the distance.

Mary nodded. She could see the island plainly enough and was content to take her husband's word for it that the lighthouse was there too.

"Would you like to go over one day?"

"I can't say I've thought much about it, but yes now that you mention it, it might be fun to do that if the weather was good. Mind you, as you well know, I'm not much of a sailor so the sea would have to be dead calm."

"Well, then, maybe we'll go one day next summer. I'm told the boat leaves from Ballycastle. Do you think Molly might come too?"

"She might. Our Molly's always a great one for an outing."

"Well, let's ask her when we get to Ballycastle."

"Aye, we'll do that."

"Oh darling, would you look at that?" he said, this time pointing in the distance to a small white church silhouetted against the morning sky. She could see it now sitting high above the cliffs overlooking the sea. She held it in her gaze for as long as she could while the car coasted the rest of the way down the road and stopped in the centre of the village.

Other than the smoke rising from the chimneys of two small houses the village appeared deserted. On the other side of the road a thatched cottage stood abandoned and in ruins. The roof had collapsed and fallen into the house. Most of the windows were broken leaving jagged edges of glass embedded in the window frames. And in the yard a rusting piece of farm equipment was overgrown by nettles. Only the metal seat was visible above the tall nettles and weeds that surrounded the house. Thompson glanced at the sea, then back at the ruined cottage and wondered how many generations had lived in this place and how many of them had worked the small farm or left their home to seek a better life in some far off land, perhaps never to return. And for no reason at all, he found himself hoping they'd lived a good life.

The car moved forward a short distance before turning into the winding road that led to Dunseverick harbour. It had been awhile since he had been there and he had forgotten just how narrow the road was and how closely it ran to the edge of the steep grassy cliffs that dropped several hundred feet to the shoreline below. There was barely room for two cars to pass and he was relieved that no one was coming the other way. As they started down the narrow road above the harbour he could see once more the headland at Ballintoy and the small white church keeping its solitary watch. At the bottom of the hill the road widened into a small parking area directly above the harbour.

Together they sat watching the sea breaking over the rocks that sheltered the small harbour. A large wave crashed against the end of the concrete breakwater sending a column of white water high into the air. Three open fishing boats supported on small wooden cradles sat on the concrete slipway high above the waterline. One of the boats had been freshly varnished and the gunnels painted a brilliant green. Above them they could hear the plaintive cry of gulls as they circled high overhead.

Mary was glad that she'd agreed to come. "It's so peaceful here," she said gently squeezing his hand.

"Aye it is.... I've often thought it would be nice to have a wee house in a place like this, nothing fancy mind you, no more than a cottage really with a bedroom and an open fire in the kitchen. Over there, on that flat piece of high ground overlooking the sea," he pointed to a spot on the other side of the harbour.

"Oh, it's a lovely spot right enough, but I think you might find it terribly lonely."

"Perhaps that's the beauty of the place..."

"All the same, I think you'd change your mind after a winter of it." She had been born in County Galway and knew better than most what it was like to live on the coast in the middle of winter with nothing but wind and rain as constant companions.

"Aye, well, you should know, I'll grant you that. Still, there's something about this place that has always drawn me to it. I was aware of it the first time my uncle brought me here on his motorbike. I remember that day for I was barely big enough to hold on and my uncle made me sit on top of the petrol tank between his arms. I've never been able to put my finger on it, but it's a powerful feeling all the same. I know my uncle felt it too for he talked about it often. And do you know, Mary, I don't think I've ever experienced this feeling anywhere else. It's as if somehow this is where I belong."

Thompson looked across the harbour to the steep rocks that rose above the breakwater, and just for a moment, wanted more than anything to fling open the car door and scamper up over the rocks to the small green meadow and the stretch of golden sand that lay hidden on the other side, to a secret place, a place he had discovered as a young boy and claimed as his own. It was a place, he remembered, where he stood looking out to sea in search of a world that existed only in his own imagination.

He felt his wife's hand on his shoulder. "Willie, darling, I think we'd better go now."

"Hmm....what did you say?"

"I said, I think we should go, it's getting on."

"Aye.... aye, perhaps we should."

Reluctantly, he released the handbrake and the car started back up the narrow winding road. For a time he said nothing, preferring instead to keep his own council and to ponder the contentment he felt inside.

Chapter Twelve

They arrived in Ballycastle just before noon. The town was quiet as it was on most Sunday mornings. At this time of the morning ordinary working people were at home gathered around the kitchen table or in bed enjoying the one day in the week that was theirs to do with as they pleased. Those who had ventured out to church were still there. Only an occasional car passed them on the street as they made their way down into the centre of the town. As they passed the harbour, a few of the older men, mostly fishermen, could be seen milling about the pier as they did each Sunday morning when the weather was fair. They gathered to share a pipe of tobacco and to exchange stories about the sea and the events of the past week or whatever else took their fancy. They were humorous men who enjoyed telling a good yarn at the expense of an unsuspecting tourist when the opportunity presented itself.

"It looks peaceful enough."

"Aye, it does... you'd never think there was anything wrong.

"No...no you wouldn't."

At Bernardo's Orphanage the car slowed, turned the corner and stopped. A few yards farther up the road a police constable was standing in the middle of the street waving them back. Behind him a Land-Rover had been pulled across the road blocking further access to the street. Thompson rolled down his window as the young man approached.

"I'm sorry, sir, but I must ask you to turn back," he said firmly. He paused for a moment then walked to the rear of the car and directed Thompson back onto the main street that ran through the town. The young constable returned to the driver's window and lowered his head to look into the car. "Perhaps, I can help you find an alternate route, sir."

"Oh, no need Constable. The street we want is handy enough. It was just shorter for us to go this way that's all. We're over from Coleraine visiting our daughter," Thompson said with just a hint of nervousness in his voice. "But thanks all the same."

"Good day to you both, then."

"And to you constable."

"Constable... I'm sorry for your trouble." Thompson heard his wife say, quite unexpectedly.

The young policeman hesitated for a moment as if searching for the right thing to say. "That's very thoughtful of you to say so madam....thank you." He turned from the car and walked hurriedly away.

"God love him, he looks so young," Mary said, shaking her head at the senselessness of it all.

"Aye.... sure, he's only a youngster."

"God help him, I'd be worried sick if he was one of mine."

"Oh, I'm sure his own mother does plenty of that."

"I'm certain she does, for what mother wouldn't."

"Aye, that's true."

"It's sad to see it all starting again. I had hoped we'd put this kind of thing behind us....God knows over the years we've had more than our share of trouble in this wee country of ours," Mary said.

"I think we'd all hoped that."

The car turned and moved cautiously forward. A few minutes later Thompson drove into a quiet residential street not far from the strand. He parked the car in front of a small two storey house set back from the street by an enclosed front lawn that badly needed attention. Maybe that was something he could do the next time he came to the house, he thought, it would be one less thing Molly would have to worry about.

"Well, love, we're here."

"We are indeed," she said cheerfully, getting out of the car and walking over to the small iron gate. She opened the gate and waited for her husband to catch up. Together they walked the short distance to the front entrance, rang the door bell and waited for Molly to appear.

"You'll be ready for that cup of tea, now."

"Aye... I will."

"Oh, I'm sure Molly will put the kettle on soon enough. She knows how fond her father is of his tea."

Thompson waited for a few minutes before walking over to the bay window to have a peek inside. The lights were on in the front room and in the hall, but there was no sign of anyone. She must be upstairs, he thought, as he reached over and rang the door bell a second time.

"That's strange. She's always home at this time on a Sunday morning. I don't know where she could be."

"I don't know either Mary, unless she's gone for a walk with the youngster."

"I hardly think so, not at dinner time."

"I don't know what to say."

"No... nor I."

"Well, let's wait in the car. I'm sure she'll be along any minute."

"Willie... you don't think something happened?"

"Would you have an ounce of sense woman. What in God's

139

name could have happened to her?"

"Don't be angry. It's just that I find it odd she's not here."

"I'm not angry. I just don't want you worrying over nothing. I know what you're like. And sure, she doesn't even know we're coming. Come on now, let's wait in the car. At least you'll be warmer." He put his arm around her and together they started to walk back towards the car.

"Mister, are you looking for the woman that lives in that house."

Thompson turned to see a small boy standing on the street in front of the house next door. He hadn't noticed him before. Perhaps he had only just come out. He looked to be no more than five or six years of age.

"We are... have you seen her?"

"No, I haven't."

Thompson smiled at the youngster, and again turned back towards the car.

"My mammy says that woman was bombed."

"Oh, Dear God, Willie... What's that wee fella saying?"

"Hush woman..."

"Oh please God..."

Thompson stooped down and looked into the small boy's eyes. "Where's your mother, son?" he asked softly, his voice betraying his own fear."

"She's in the house. Two big policemen talked to her...so they did....they made her cry."

"Oooh, dear God, no... not Molly....Oh please God. Oh Holy Mother of God don't let it be our Molly," Mary screamed, burying her face in her hands.

Suddenly alarmed the small boy ran back to the safety of his own front yard.

Thompson took his wife in his arms and held her as tightly as he dared. He didn't know what to say. For a time they just stood there on the street and clung to each other.

"Oh, Willie, what are we to do...?"

"Darling, I don't know, but let's find out what's happened; maybe the wee boy's mistaken."

"Aye, that's it, sure he's only a youngster," she said, wiping her tears with a small linen handkerchief.

"There...that's better."

A woman emerged from the house next door and was standing on the front step holding her hands over her mouth. Mary recognized her immediately. It was Molly's neighbour.

"Oh you'll come in, won't you?" the woman said nervously. She too had been crying, they could see that plainly enough for her eyes were red and puffy and she looked awfully pale.

"Aye...if you don't mind," Thompson said.

"That's very thoughtful of you," Mary added, as she took her husband's hand and followed the woman into a small sitting room that overlooked the street and a small flower garden.

"Can you tell us what happened?" Mary asked, trying to hold back her tears, hoping with all her heart that the small boy was mistaken.

"I only know what they told me... you'll want to talk to them yourself. But it seems Molly was on the street last night, I think on her way home, when the bomb went off. They didn't know until late this morning who she was. They came to the house an hour ago looking for the names of relatives and that's when I told them you lived in Coleraine. I'm sorry, but I wasn't able to tell them exactly where you lived. It would have been helpful I know...."

"Och, that's not your fault. But what about little Tommy? Was the wee fellow with his mother when it happened?" Thompson asked, fearful of what she might tell him.

"Yes... I think so... they said there was a small child... Ooh I'm so sorry, Mr. Thompson and for you too Mary," she added tearfully.

"Oh dear God, where are they now?" Mary asked, no longer

able to hold back her tears.

"They've taken them to Coleraine."

"Dear God....where?"

"To the hospital..."

"You mean they're alright."

"I don't know... but I think so...I'm just not certain. All they would tell me was that they'd been rushed by ambulance to the hospital in Coleraine."

"Why didn't you say so before?"

The young woman lowered her head and began to sob pitifully.

"What's wrong mammy?" the small boy asked anxiously, pulling on his mother's sleeve.

"Oh dear God, I'm sorry... Ooh please, please forgive me, I didn't mean to be angry at you. God knows, it's not your fault...it's just that I thought the worst...I'm so sorry." Mary took the young woman in her arms and held her for what seemed like a long time. It was like holding her own daughter and at that moment it was something she desperately needed to do.

"There....there now, that will do. Sure, it'll be alright, you'll see."

She turned back to her husband, tears streaming down her face." Willie darling, did you hear what she said? Molly and Tommy are in the hospital. Thanks be to God."

He could only nod through his own tears. "Aye love, I did... I did," he whispered almost inaudibly.

"Ooh, thank God... at least they're alive. I thought for a minute we'd lost them... and dear God, for now, that's all that matters."

As they turned to walk back out to the street Thompson patted the small boy gently on the head. "There now son, go on in and look after your mammy like a good wee fellow."

Chapter Thirteen

Father Nolan waited for the other man to say something as he pulled his black cassock above his ankles and stretched his tired old legs out in front of him. Standing to celebrate the Mass seemed to take more out of him these days and he was always glad to sit down in a comfortable chair as soon as it was convenient to do so. It was one of the reasons he didn't always spend as much time as he should greeting people at the door as they left the chapel.

They had agreed to meet in the parochial house after mass. At one point, while he was waiting, it occurred to the Inspector it might be interesting to slip quietly into the back of the chapel and find a seat close to the door where no one would notice him, although he had to admit it was unlikely his presence would go unnoticed. In a small tightly knit community like this he was likely to stick out like a sore thumb. He had never been to a Catholic mass and was curious to know if the stories he'd heard were true. When he first entered the chapel earlier in the morning, in search of Father Nolan, the sweet smell of incense that lingered in the damp morning air made him feel strangely uncomfortable. And the large ornate statue of the Virgin Mary towering over rows of empty pews only served to heighten his discomfort. No, the chapel was no place for him.

"Sir, I want to say how grateful I am you're willing to help. I'm afraid not everyone would you know. The truth is it's becoming more and more difficult for the police to get the cooperation they need from the community. Sadly, even good people now seem reluctant to step forward. It wasn't always that way mind you, but times have changed and we do the best we can, thankful for whatever help we get," Inspector Hamill said solemnly, as he sat down opposite the old man who had already taken his seat in front of the fire.

"Well, of course, I'm willing to do what I can," he said, handing the policeman a cup of tea from a freshly brewed pot.

"It's much appreciated, sir."

"Perhaps you'd care for sugar."

"No, but I'll take a wee drop of milk."

"Feel free to smoke if you like, Inspector."

He went through the motions of searching for a cigarette. "I would, but I seemed to have misplaced mine," he added, looking at the other man hopefully.

"Thanks, but I don't smoke, sir."

"And not much of a drinker either, I'll wager."

"Only occasionally, sir."

"Well now, how can I help you? And to be frank Inspector, I'm not at all sure I can. I don't know what it is you think I can do to assist in your investigation."

"Sir, I think that will become apparent in a moment. It's just a question of knowing where to begin."

"Inspector Hamill... you did say Hamill, did you not?"

"Yes, Sir, I did."

"Well Inspector, if you want my help, I would suggest a good place to start might be at the beginning."

"Quite right, sir."

144

He tapped his lips with his finger as he tried to decide just how much information should be shared with the man sitting opposite him, who was already growing impatient with the measured pace of the conversation. There was always the risk of disclosing too much information especially at the beginning. It was a delicate matter at the best of times and in the end it came down to how much confidence he was prepared to place in the wily old priest or how much he was prepared to gamble to get what he needed. He knew too, that in this part of the country the I.R.A. had a significant number of people sympathetic to their cause, some even among the Catholic clergy. Father Nolan was nobody's fool. He could see that clearly enough, and he was just as certain the old man would not suffer fools gladly.

"Well, man... out with it."

"It has to do with the lorry...the army lorry I mentioned when we met briefly in the chapel."

"Aye, that much I gathered."

"We think the lorry may be connected to the bombing in Ballycastle. A lorry bearing the same description was stopped at a police road block in Bushmills last night. We can't be sure of course, it's a bit too early to tell, but it looks as if the two incidents might be related. It's hard to fathom what the lorry was doing on that part of the road. It seems the driver may have lost control of the vehicle and from what I've been told very nearly ended up in the sea."

"Dear God!"

"A local Cushendun man found the burned-out wreck very early this morning. One man was found dead, still in the overturned lorry and horribly burned. It will take some time of course before forensics will be able to identify the remains. The second man was fortunately thrown clear and found lying by the side of the road several yards from where the lorry veered off the pavement and plunged down a rocky embankment. He's badly hurt, but alive at least for now, and he has asked to speak to his parish priest. And that's where you come in, Father. He's asking for you."

"Are you quite certain?"

"I am."

"Did he tell you his name?"

"No...no he didn't, but then they seldom do. He's only a young fellow, perhaps in over his head and maybe even looking for a way out. I can't be sure, of course, but by the look of him I've a hunch that might be the case. It's not often we're this fortunate and so we're hoping he may be able to provide us with enough information to sort out what may have happened and to determine whether the incident with the lorry is connected to the bombing in Ballycastle. I'd like you to talk to him about that if you can. We'll deal with him ourselves, of course, but that always takes time and even then there's no guarantee he'll say anything. We think he might say something to you that would help us finger the people responsible...."

"I'm a parish priest, not a bloody informer," the old priest said angrily.

"I am sorry you feel that way," the Inspector snapped back, trying to contain his own anger at the priest's sudden outburst. "Not to put too fine a point on it, sir, but I hardly think the families who have lost loved ones over the past few months to sectarian violence will share your sensitivity. And tell me this Father, if decent men like yourself won't speak out against this madness, who will?"

Both men glared at each other and for an awkward moment neither of them was quite sure just what to do or say next.

The Inspector was the first to speak for the priest appeared to be in no hurry to resume the conversation. "I'm sorry, sir... I'm afraid I've gone too far," the policeman said, in an effort to ease the tension between them.

"Oh, let it go... there's no need for an apology."

"No... no there is. I had no right to speak to you in that way.

It's just that when you see what I see ....well... to tell you the the truth it's sometimes difficult to deal with."

"Och, sure there's no need to say anymore. You're only doing your job and sure the police have every right to expect decent people to come forward when innocent people are being killed by a bunch of bloody hooligans regardless of what side they're on. No wonder Ireland is in the sorry state it's in."

"I take it then, you'll do what you can."

"Aye, well I'll certainly see him."

"I'm deeply grateful to you."

"Then perhaps we best get on with it."

"Yes, you're quite right, sir."

"When would you like me to speak to the young fellow?"

"Father, if it's convenient, I'd rather hoped you'd do it right away."

"You mean now...this afternoon?"

"Yes...if at all possible."

"You don't waste any time, Inspector."

"I'm afraid, I can't afford to, there's really no telling how long we might have."

"No, I don't suppose there is."

The policeman rose to his feet and set the empty cup and saucer on the small table. "It will mean driving to Ballymena, I'm afraid. The lad's been taken to the hospital there, although I understand he may have to be transferred to the Royal in Belfast as soon as he can be moved. I'm told his condition is extremely serious, which only adds to the urgency in getting you there as quickly as possible. I'm sure you understand."

The old priest nodded, "Well, then, I suppose we'd better get started," he said, pulling himself up from the chair. "The truth is Inspector, I'd just as soon get it over with."

"I understand, sir, but with any luck we'll have you back in Cushendall by mid afternoon. I have a car standing by to take us as soon as you're ready to leave. I thought that would be more convenient for you."

"Aye, well, just give me a minute."

"By all means, sir"

"Good God, man, I almost forgot. I had better leave a note for my housekeeper. There'll be the devil to pay if I don't."

"Sir..."

"What is it Inspector...is there something wrong?"

"No, it's just that I would ask you to keep the matter strictly to yourself. I'm sure you understand."

"Oh, don't worry Inspector. Believe me, Mrs Cassidy's the last woman in the world I'd want to tell anything to."

A short time later an unmarked police car pulled out of the driveway and accelerated down the road. In the back seat, Father Nolan laid his head back and closed his eyes. His thoughts turned to the young man who had asked to see a priest and to his parents who were probably even now unaware of what had happened; probably ordinary people caught up in a web of violence that was not of their making. He wondered too how men with murder in their hearts could fail to consider the consequences of what they were doing. "God what a terrible thing," he heard himself mutter.

"Did you say something, sir?"

"No... no, I don't think so... I was just thinking out loud."

"Would you care for a cigarette?"

"Aye... I could use one, right enough."

"The constable's a smoker like yourself," the inspector added, smiling at the priest in the rear view mirror as he reached back and passed him the pack of cigarettes.

"I'm much obliged, constable."

"Oh, don't mention it, sir."

They were on the main road to Ballymena now and the car's speed increased alarmingly. The old priest couldn't remember driving this fast in his whole life and was more grateful than ever for the cigarette they had given him just moments earlier. The driver wasn't wasting any time and it crossed his mind that if they drove any faster he would need more than a few cigarettes to steady himself. A good belt of whiskey would certainly help, but it occurred to him that asking for a drink in the back of a police car was probably unwise.

"At this speed it won't take us that long," he heard the Inspector say reassuringly from the front seat.

"No, I don't suppose it will," the priest replied nervously.

"Father, when you finish your cigarette go ahead and make yourself comfortable. It won't bother us if you decide to put your head back and catch a few minutes sleep."

"Well Inspector, if it's all the same to you, I would just as soon sit upright and watch the countryside fly by, for God knows it's flying past at a terrible rate."

The drive to Ballymena was no more than twenty miles. A short time later the car entered the town and within minutes pulled into the back parking lot of the hospital, stopping beside several other police vehicles.

"We're here, sir," the Inspector said, stepping out of the car to hold the rear door open.

The old priest hesitated.

"Sir, are you alright? You're looking a bit pale."

"Aye....aye, the best."

"Here... let me help you."

"Och, there's no need."

"Sir, I know these things are never easy," the Inspector said, taking the old priest's arm and helping him to his feet.

The old man didn't bother to reply.

"It's just that without your help we're not likely to get very far. Believe me I appreciate, what you are doing."

"I haven't done anything yet."

"No, but you will..."

"You seem rather sure of that."

"I am."

"Well, I'll do what I can."

"Sir, if it's any comfort, I meant what I said earlier. Not everyone would want to be bothered with this kind of thing and some would even go out of their way to make things difficult for the police."

"Inspector, I don't know who your man is in there or for that matter what he's done. But I'll tell you one thing. There's no doubt in my mind why I'm here. The young fellow asked to see a priest and God help me that's what I am. I'll do what I can to help of course, I said I would. I just want that understood."

The priest lowered his head and held his weathered brow in his hand. His grey hair fell forward covering one side of his face. Pushing it back he ran his fingers through the thick mop of unkempt hair. He was an old man and this afternoon he felt his age more than usual. In all his years in the priesthood he had never before been asked to assist the police in this way. It was the right thing to do, of course, but somehow that didn't make it any easier.

"Inspector, there's something else you should be clear about."

"Sir, if I may..."

"Please... please let me finish."

"I'm sorry. I didn't mean to interrupt."

"Well, it's just that you should be aware I'll not disclose anything the man might say in making his confession, however useful it might be to your investigation."

"Sir... I am aware of that."

"Good, then, that's settled."

Inside the vestibule they were met by the matron, a large woman with a commanding presence. "Good afternoon, Inspector, we've been expecting you... do come and sit down," she said loudly, gesturing to a number of comfortable chairs in the waiting room across the hall.

"Matron, I'd like you to meet Father Nolan."

"Ah yes...and a good afternoon to you Father. Would you like

150

me to arrange for some tea and perhaps a wee biscuit or two?"

"That's very kind of you, but no thanks matron."

"You're quite sure."

"I am."

"And what about you, Inspector?"

"Thanks, but no, I won't bother either."

"I suppose then, you'd like to see the patient without further delay."

"Yes...yes, indeed matron," the Inspector said, rising to his feet.

The matron led them down a wide corridor and up one flight of stairs to the next floor. On the second level they walked quickly to the end of a lighted corridor where two police constables stood outside the door of what appeared to be a private ward.

"I'll leave you then, Inspector."

"Yes, if you would matron."

As she turned to leave, she heard the old priest call after her.

"Yes...Father what is it?"

"Oh, it's just that I meant to ask you how the lad's doing...it would be helpful to know that before I see him."

The matron hesitated. "Poorly I'm afraid, his condition appears to be worse than we first thought. Sadly, I don't think there's much more we can do," she said shaking her head. "He's very anxious to see you Father, and he refuses to talk to anyone, even the nursing sisters."

"I see...well, thank you for telling me that."

"We've made him as comfortable as we can, of course."

"Oh, I'm quite sure you have."

"Well, if there's nothing else, Inspector."

"No, there's nothing, thank you, matron."

The matron turned and quickly retraced her steps down the long corridor towards the stairs they had climbed a few minutes earlier.

"Sir, if you don't mind I thought I'd wait for you downstairs in the waiting room."

"Aye, perhaps that would be just as well."

"By the way, sir, should you need assistance, just let one of the constables here know."

"Thank you... I will."

One of the constables nodded politely as he held the door open to allow Father Nolan to enter the room. The door closed behind him and he found himself in a large, dreary room. There was a strong odour of disinfectant that seemed to permeate everything in the room. The blinds on the window were drawn, allowing only a small shaft of sunlight to penetrate the dimly lit space. The walls were painted a nondescript green colour that reminded him of public buildings he had seen in other parts of Ireland, particularly in the north. The paint had faded and in places peeled off the wall altogether, revealing patches of greying plaster. He picked up a chair and slowly carried it to the side of the bed. The man lying in the bed appeared to be in his mid twenties, perhaps even younger. It was difficult to tell because of the large dressing that covered most of his head. He lay very still, his breathing shallow and irregular. The old priest shook his head in silent protest, wondering again, why Ireland was so bent on its own destruction and why his God was so longsuffering. He sat in silence, uncertain as to whether the other man was even aware of his presence. The room was unbearably warm and already he was feeling uncomfortable in the heavy overcoat he had worn for the journey. Unable to stand the heat any longer, he stood up and hastily removed his scarf and overcoat and threw them on the floor beside the chair. It was then he saw the young man turn his head and open first one eye and then the other before briefly closing them again.

"Father Nolan..."

"Yes, my son."

"Is it really you, Father?"

"Aye, it's me, son....you asked to see me."

"I did...aye, I did."

"Do I know you? I can't say I recognize you."

"I'm not surprised, not in this state."

"Who are you, son?"

"I'm Jimmy...Jimmy Draper."

"Jimmy Draper?"

"Aye, Sammy Draper's...."

"Och dear God, you're Sammy Draper's wee fella."

"I am."

"Who would have believed it? Sure I know your mother and father well."

"Aye....aye, I know you do."

"Mind you, I haven't seen your father since he moved the boat to Carnlough, it must be a good three or four years."

"More like five."

"I can hardly believe it's been that long."

"Oh it's been a good five years, Father."

"I don't know where the time goes. How old are you now, son?"

"I'm twenty-two... twenty-three next April."

"Oh, son, how did you ever get mixed up in the likes of this?"

"I don't know Father... it seemed the right thing to do at the time."

"You don't seem that sure."

"No... no you're right, but it's a bit late now. I'm an I.R.A. man, you know."

The old priest shook his head.

"Well, I am....I mean I was."

"Oh, I wouldn't say it too loudly, not with those two fellows standing on the other side the door."

"F.... them!"

"We'll have none of that, mind your tongue, now."

"Aye, well that's how I feel."

"I won't have it...do you hear?"

The young man hesitated before he answered. "I'm sorry, Father...it just slipped out of me."

"And well you should be."

"Father, I need your help...."

The young man closed his eyes and sighed deeply. His face, or what the old priest could see of it, was pale and drawn, beads of sweat covered his forehead and ran down his cheek.

"Son...are you alright?"

He opened his eyes and speaking almost in a whisper turned to face Father Nolan. "The thing is, Father... they don't know... they don't know I'm a member of the I.R.A."

"Who doesn't know?"

"My parents, who else? And to make things worse, my poor ma's not that well...when she finds out, it'll break her heart."

"Oh, it might..."

"Ooh, it will...I'm sure of it."

"Well, maybe you should've thought of that before, son."

"Aye, maybe so... and that's why I need you to make it right, Father."

"God knows, I wish it were that easy, son."

The old priest reached across the bed and gently touched the young man's shoulder. "Son, maybe this is as good a time as any for me to hear your confession."

"I don't mean to offend you Father, but I'd just as soon not bother if it's all the same to you. The truth is I've never been much of a Catholic. And I'm not sure now that I believe much in anything. No, that's not why I sent for you."

"In the name of God, what then?"

"I need you to speak to my parents," he whispered, his voice growing weaker than before. "Father promise me you'll do that."

"And just what is it you expect me to tell them, Jimmy."

"Tell them I've left that crowd....tell them I made a mistake and tell them I'm sorry."

"Son, listen..."

"No, Father. You listen. Tell them I meant no harm. I only did it because I believed it was the right thing to do.... nothing else seems to have worked, we all know that. I thought I could help our cause."

"Did you now, and what bloody cause would that be, can you tell me that?" the old man said, raising his voice in anger and immediately regretting it.

"Och think what you like Father, but I swear to you I never thought there would be any killing... it's not right, I know that now. And last night all we were supposed to do was get rid of the lorry. But it went badly wrong."

"God help you, Jimmy, what have you done?"

"Oh enough...."

"Jimmy, listen."

"What...."

"Son, do you not think you should talk to the police."

"I can't do that..."

"Dear God man, don't you know you're in terrible trouble?"

"Oh... I do, but I'm too tired to care."

"Well...maybe you should rest now, I can always come back."

"No...no, please stay where you are. There'll be time to rest soon enough. I need to know you'll do what I've asked you. Father, you will, won't you?"

"I'll do what I can, I will son."

"I won't forget what you've done, Father."

"No, I don't suppose you will... I know I won't."

"Jimmy," the old priest hesitated before continuing, "look son, it's not for me to tell you what do, but you might be wise to speak to the police."

"And help those ....

"Watch what you say now."

"I didn't say it father."

"No, but it wasn't far from the tip of your tongue."

"And why should I tell them anything....can you tell me that?"

"Oh, I'm not sure that I can, son. But I know this, there are times when we have to search our own hearts to know what we should do. And I'll tell you something else you might want to think about; if you speak up now, you might prevent the senseless killing of more innocent people. Didn't you just finish telling me it was the killing that bothered you the most. And one last thing son; it may be the only chance you'll get to set things right. You might want to think about that too."

The young man turned slowly away and stared blankly at the drab green wall just inches from his head. For several minutes no one spoke. The old priest lowered his head and closing his eyes wondered what would become of the young man in the unlikely event he survived his injuries. He looked so young, much younger than his twenty-two years. Too young, he thought, to be mixed up in something this terrible. He wondered too, what he would say to his parents and how they would take the news that their son was a member of the I.R.A. That was something he would have to sort out later. He started to say something, but thought better of it. The truth was he had probably said enough. Jimmy would have to make up his own mind.

"Father...can you hear me?"

"Aye...what is it son?"

"Maybe you're right Father, but I won't talk to them....I can't do that... but you can," the young man said, his voice barely audible, his breathing more laboured than before. "I don't think I have much time left Father," he added, slowly turning to face the priest who had now moved closer to the bed.

Father Nolan listened patiently to what the young man had to say. A short time later he offered up a silent prayer, picked up his coat and scarf from the floor and quietly left the room, shaken by what he had heard.

"Father, the Inspector's waiting for you downstairs and the matron asked one of the sisters to make a wee cup of tea. You look as if you could use a cup. This way sir," the constable said, pointing toward the stairs at the far end of the corridor.

Exhausted, Father Nolan followed at his own pace. The whole ordeal had taken a great deal out of him, certainly more than he had anticipated. He was thankful it was over and at that moment wanted nothing more than to be back in Cushendall. Perhaps there he might be able to make some sense out of all he had heard, although he had to admit, that seemed highly unlikely.

"Ah, here we are, and just in time by the look of things. Thank you sister," the matron said, taking the tea tray from a young nursing sister who had entered the waiting room.

"Sir, do sit down and make yourself comfortable. I know you must be anxious to get back to Cushendall. Are you sure you're alright, Father? You look as if you've had more than enough for one day, if you don't mind me saying so," the Inspector said, rising to his feet and pointing to an empty chair.

"Aye, indeed I have."

"Matron, perhaps you could leave us now."

"Of course, Inspector. If you need anything else you know where to find me."

"I do; thanks very much for your help."

"I'll say goodbye to both of you, then."

The matron closed the door behind her leaving the two men alone in the small room.

"You will have a cup Father?"

"Aye, I will... and a cigarette too, if you can find one," he said.

"I thought you might," the Inspector said, handing him a new pack of cigarettes and a box of matches.

"That's very thoughtful of you."

"No, not at all... it's the least we can do."

Father Nolan drank a mouthful of hot tea and set the cup back down on the table directly in front of him. He eagerly lit a cigarette and lowered his head on the back of the chair.

"Sir, I won't keep you long. I know you want to be on your way," the Inspector said, taking a small black notebook and a pen from the inside pocket of his blazer.

"I'd be much obliged, Inspector."

"Well sir, perhaps we could get started."

"Aye..." he replied wearily.

"It would be helpful if you could tell me everything he said, or as much as you're at liberty to tell. I haven't forgotten our earlier conversation."

"Well, as it turns out, there's really nothing I can't share with you. He won't speak to the police himself, but he wants me to tell you what he's told me. I think it's the only way he knows to set things right."

"Good, and remember Father, in this business, sometimes seemingly insignificant things can turn out to be very important."

The old priest nodded.

For the next twenty minutes Inspector Hamill listened carefully as the old priest related the conversation he'd had a short time earlier, interrupting him only occasionally to clarify something that had been said. When he had finished, the Inspector closed the notebook and tapped it lightly with his pen. He had been right to confide in Father Nolan; indeed, the old priest had turned out to be quite a remarkable man.

"You're quite sure he said Meagher."

"I am. He said it several times."

"Well... well, at least we now know where he is or more likely where he's been," the Inspector said solemnly.

"If there's nothing else I'd prefer to be on my way."

"Yes, of course."

"Then, I'll leave you, Inspector. You'll have things to do I'm sure."

"Sir, the car's waiting outside to take you back."

"Goodbye, Inspector."

"Goodbye Father and I do want to thank you."

"Please..." the old priest said, holding up his hand in protest.

He hadn't noticed it before, but as the old man prepared to

158

leave, the policeman saw the anguish in his eyes. "Sir, I don't think you realize just how helpful you've been."

The old priest didn't reply.

"Let me walk you to the car."

"If you don't mind, Inspector, I'd just as soon see myself out."

"Very well, sir."

He got to his feet with some difficulty and stood for a few moments steadying himself against the back of the chair before making his way to the door.

"Oh there is one other thing you ought to know Inspector. I'm afraid in all the commotion it quite slipped my mind, although, for the life of me, I don't know why it should. Perhaps it's something I would just as soon forget, but it's something you need to know. Your man in there seems quite certain that what happened in Ballycastle is only the beginning of something far more terrible. God forbid it should come to that."

Chapter Fourteen

Hand in hand they walked leisurely up the Mountsandel road as far as Warnock's Lane. The young man removed his raincoat and laid it on the grass with the lining down to avoid getting stains on the outside of the coat. Earlier in the week, his mother had made a point of asking how he managed to get grass stains on the new raincoat she'd bought only a month ago and was now paying for on the weekly instalment plan. The question had taken him by surprise and the explanation he'd given on the spur of the moment, he knew from the look on her face, was less than convincing. Fortunately she had let it go at that probably knowing full well how it had happened and perhaps even remembering that she too had once been young. His mother was no fool and he thought it best to be more careful in future. It wasn't that he was careless or unaware of how difficult it was sometimes for his parents to make ends meet. It was just that it was hard to know what else to do when you wanted to lie in the grass with your girl. It was a common practice and part of the courting ritual in Ireland.

The air was turning colder and the grass felt damp from the rain of the previous day. The hedge and stand of trees that lined both sides of the lane offered some shelter from the gusts of wind that rose and moved across the open fields. Where they were was the best spot in the lane, for here a small grove of evergreens hid them from the prying eyes of passers by. They had found it on one of their first long walks together. Others had found it too for sometimes the grass was already flattened when they lay down together. It was called a lane, but it was really a narrow road that ran between Mountsandel and the main road to Ballymoney. Now, with the change in the weather their visits were becoming less frequent and they both knew it would soon be too cold and wet to spend much time together outdoors. Even now the weather was noticeably colder. Sometimes they stayed in the town and held each other behind the high stone wall of the Irish Society School which was only a short distance from where she lived. It wasn't a very private place and small boys, including his own younger brother, often climbed the wall to spy on them or make a nuisance of themselves. The young man wished he had the use of a car, but his family couldn't afford one and it was highly unlikely they would ever be in a position to own one. Only once had he taken her to his house when his parents were off down the town, but he was so nervous they might be discovered that they stayed only for a few minutes, just long enough to hold her around the waist and kiss her gently on the lips. It was something he knew he wasn't supposed to do although no one had ever said so in so many words. And before they left he cautiously stuck his head out the door to make sure no one was on the street.

On Saturday afternoons when he managed to scrape up enough money, and that wasn't very often, they went to the matinee at the local picture house and sat in the balcony with other young couples who had come with the same thing on their mind. Most of the balcony crowd were boarding school students from the Coleraine Inst and girls from the Coleraine High School. Some of the boys were proper toffs and took delight in showing off at the slightest provocation, often belittling those who were not as well off as themselves. They always seemed to have tons of money and loaded themselves down with sweets on the way in the door. Of the two cinemas in the town most young couples preferred the Palladium. There the balcony was much larger, and in the darkness the usher didn't bother anyone. They knew well enough what was going on, but they made a point of leaving well enough alone. But at Christie's picture house the owner himself often patrolled the balcony to make sure couples were behaving themselves. Admission to both cinemas cost almost two shillings, four shillings really, for it was generally accepted that the boy should pay for both tickets. It was a lot of money and if you were from a working class family it took a while to save it up from the modest weekly allowance you might be lucky enough to receive from your father or mother. There were cheaper seats, of course, in the middle section of the cinema, and if you were willing to sit closer to the screen the seats were even cheaper, but that was no place to take your girl especially if you were looking for a bit of fun.

He sometimes wished they were both older, and often wondered just how old they would have to be before they could be seen together in public without anyone taking particular notice of them. Lying in bed one morning he tried to figure out just how old he would have to be before he could take her hand and walk down Church Street, or any other street in the town for that matter. He was only fifteen when he first met her and he knew that was too young. But now that he was sixteen he didn't think that was old enough either, maybe on his next birthday it would be alright....and if he were eighteen, surely then, they could go wherever they pleased without much bother. Perhaps he might even bring her into the house without worrying about what the neighbours might say, but maybe that was expecting too much, even if she weren't a Roman Catholic.

He loved her and he had told her so.

The young couple lay huddled together enjoying the warmth of each others' bodies. He kissed her and she kissed him back. She moved herself closer and he felt the softness of her young body through her winter coat. He pushed himself against her and as he did so he knew she was aware of him for she moved her firm young body even closer and kissed him with her open mouth. They had never before allowed themselves to become this intimate and it made them giddy with excitement. Out of breath they rolled on their backs and lay peeking through the low overhanging branches at a patch of grey overcast sky.

"Oh, I love you," she said excitedly. "I do you know. I love you... There, I said it again. Now I want to hear you say it."

"You're being silly, Aggie."

"No. I want to hear you say it."

"Why?"

"Because."

"Och, you are silly."

"I am not."

"Yes, you are."

"I want you to say it."

"I love you.... there I said it you silly thing."

"Again."

"Aggie...."

"No, I want to hear you say it again."

"I love you... there I did it, I said it again."

"I love you, I love you, I love you almighty. I wish your pyjamas were close to my nightie. Now don't get excited and don't be misled, I mean on the clothes line and not on the bed," she said, in a playful voice, turning her head to look directly into his eyes.

"You're daft."

"I'm daft about you."

"You're also a tease."

"Oh, you poor boy, did that excite you?"

"Yes... yes it did," he replied.

"Ooh... you poor thing."

"You know it did."

"She kissed him again, but this time more gently.

"Aggie," he said quietly.

"Yes, David."

"Oh, I just wondered if you know how I feel when we're together like this. I mean...well you know what I mean...the way we were a few minutes ago."

"Yes...of course I do.... don't you think I feel the same way?"

"I wasn't sure that girls felt that way."

"Well, they do....at least I do."

"Can I ask you something, then...?"

"If you like..."

"Do you ever think you would like to do it?"

"Ssssh." She placed her finger over his lips.

He turned his head away and her finger slipped from his mouth.

"Don't be cross with me..."

"Oh, I'm not...I just wanted to know, that's all."

"Shush."

"It's just that I've never done it...."

"I would hope not."

"Have you....?"

"No....no of course not, what a thing to ask me!"

"Never?"

"No... not ever."

"Do you ever think about doing it?"

"Yes...sometimes."

"With me?"

"Of course, silly, who else?"

"I'm glad to hear that...because that's how I feel too. I do love you Aggie."

"Oh and I love you...and we won't be sorry we waited, you'll

165

see. The priest says that's the right thing to do and that we should keep ourselves pure for it's a sin to do it before you're married.... he told us that....but somehow it didn't seem wrong when you were against me just now. It just felt wonderful."

They hugged each other as tightly as they dared until they could barely stand the pleasure and warmth they drew from each other. He pressed against her and under her coat he felt her legs open slightly as she pushed gently back against him. Only their clothing kept them apart.

The sun had gone and the air had turned noticeably colder, but they paid it no heed for they were lost in the wonder and excitement of each other.

A short time later the young man sat upright and watched a line of dark ominous clouds begin to cover the late afternoon sky. They were heavy with rain and cast a lengthening shadow on the land. The rain, he knew, was not far away. The young man looked at the young woman and in his heart he knew he loved her. He knew too, that he didn't care what others thought. And why should he? As if it mattered to him that she was a Roman Catholic. His father, he remembered, had seen them together once as he drove passed on the back of an open lorry with other tradesmen who worked for the same building contractor, but he wisely hadn't mentioned it in the house. It was the kind of thing he had come to expect of his father for he was a kind and tolerant man. His mother on the other hand, had been less tolerant when she found out who he was keeping company with and told him in no uncertain terms he should find someone of his own kind.

"A penny for your thoughts."

"They're worth more than a penny."

"How much?"

"A lot more than you have and anyway, thoughts are private things."

"Yes, but people in love are supposed to share things.... even their most private thoughts. They do...don't they?"

"I suppose so."

"Well, then."

"Oh, sssh."

"I will not."

"Oh, be quiet, silly."

"Were you thinking about us?"

"Of course..."

"Was it a nice thought?"

"Yes....yes it was," he said hesitantly, unwilling to spoil their happiness by telling her what he had really been thinking or what his mother had said about finding one of his own kind. He glanced at her and wondered again what would happen when they were old enough to get married. They had talked about that too and the difficulties they might encounter as a young couple from two different religious traditions. He wasn't about to become a Catholic, nor did he expect her to become a Protestant. When the time came they would have to sort it out as best they could even if it meant making a fresh start in some other place where people were not so intolerant of others whose faith was different from their own. And if it came to that he thought, Canada or America might be a good place for the two of them to build a life together. A few people from Coleraine had already gone to Canada and by all accounts had discovered a country with plenty of opportunities for young people willing to work, where they didn't seem to bother one way or the other what religion a person belonged to. On his own street, a young man, just a few years older than himself, had gone to Canada and was doing well. Others he knew from the town had gone to America and one who lived not far from where he lived had gone to Australia. And just last month a close friend had immigrated to South Africa.

In the architect's office where his father had recently secured work for him as an architectural apprentice, he came across a

Canadian brochure advertising timber framed cabins. One of the pictures showed a log cabin in the Rocky Mountains surrounded by tall slender pine trees set against an expanse of brilliant blue sky that seemed to go on forever. It reminded him of a scene from the movie, *The High and the Mighty*, starring John Wayne, which he had seen while he was still at school. The picture in the brochure fascinated him and in the weeks that followed he found himself thinking more and more about Canada.

"Oh, I am glad...."

She sat up and moving closer, rested her head on his shoulder. He could smell the fresh fragrance of her perfume and he knew that for a short time it would linger on his own clothing and afterwards when he was alone it would remind him of her. He put his arm around her and kissed her lovely black hair.

"You smell so good, Aggie."

"Do you think so?" she said rubbing her cheek against his shoulder, the way a cat rubs itself against your leg.

"Aggie... it's going to rain."

"Oh, well," she said, shrugging her shoulders.

"I think we should start walking back now."

"What time is it?"

"Almost half past four."

"Oh dear, I didn't think it was that late."

"Well, it is."

"The time goes so quickly when we're together."

He reached down and took her hand in his own and gently pulled her to her feet.

"You're shivering."

"I know."

"Are you cold?"

"Yes, a little. I wasn't before, but I am now."

"You can wear my coat if you like."

"I'll do no such thing, but it's sweet of you to offer."

"Suit yourself."

"Oh, it does look like rain."

"Yes, we'd better hurry."

"Not until you kiss me."

"Again?"

"Yes...one more time."

"You're going to get us both wet."

"I don't care."

"You're daft."

"Oh hush... just kiss me."

They stood together and gently held each other until they felt the first drops of rain.

"Oh, dear, there it comes."

"I told you."

"I do love you David."

"Cross your heart and hope to die."

"Yes...I do, honestly."

"I know..."

"And you, will you always love me?

"Always..."

Chapter Fifteen

They sat together in the warm car staring at the empty street. Sitting in the car for a few minutes seemed the right thing to do. If nothing else it gave them a chance to gather up the bits and pieces of the day, a chance to sort themselves out as best they could. As they watched, a dog appeared, then disappeared as quickly through a hole in the thick hedge that lined one side of the street. Closer to the car, the hedge gave way to a painted wooden fence that enclosed the greens of the bowling club. The dog reappeared and made its way up the street towards them, sniffing the ground as it moved hurriedly from one spot to another. It stopped, raised its hind leg and watered the tufts of weeds and coarse grass that grew willy nilly along the narrow strip of unkempt soil between the pavement and the fence. The process was repeated at intervals along the street until the dog finally crossed the road and disappeared again, this time for good.

"I think we'll leave the car on the street," Thompson said wearily, as he turned off the ignition and rubbed his forehead with the palm of his hand.

"Whatever you think, dear. You know it makes no difference to me one way or the other," she said indifferently.

"Well I think I will, then... that way it'll be there when we need it."

They both fell silent and for several minutes remained lost in their own thoughts, each in their own way struggling to deal with the terrible thing that had happened. Thompson raised his head and glanced at the empty street and then at a darkening sky that was moving rapidly towards them. The scene outside only added to the dreariness of the late afternoon and heightened their mood of despair. A few drops of heavy rain, the first of the day, splattered loudly against the windshield.

"Oh dear, there's the rain," Mary said, with a quiet sigh.

"Aye... and it looks as if it might settle in for the evening."

"Indeed it does....."

He reached across the seat and tenderly took his wife's small hand in his own. "Mary, I was just thinking that when we started off this morning who would have thought a day that began with such promise would end like this."

"God knows, that's the truth, but sure none of us know what a day will bring."

"No... but who would have expected anything like this? This is the kind of thing that happens to other families, but never to your own or at least that's what we like to tell ourselves."

"Aye, we like to think that. My mother used to say it's a good thing none of us know what lies ahead of us. Mind you, when it happens it doesn't make it any easier, does it?"

"No it doesn't."

"Oh, dear God, Willie....what are we to do?"

"Hush, love, sure we'll be alright, you'll see." He kissed her lightly on the forehead. "There now, that's better. I think maybe we had better go inside. It's beginning to rain a lot heavier and it's getting colder."

"What a pity," she said softly, drying the rest of her tears with a small silk handkerchief. "I thought we might have an early supper, and afterwards walk back to the hospital. It's not that far and the walk would do us both good. Don't you think?"

"It probably would... we'll wait and see, then. It may only be a shower after all although by the look of it I'd say that's not too likely."

"You may be right."

"Oh well, sure we can walk anyway. It's not as if the rain's likely to do us much harm; we've lived with it long enough to know that."

Mary smiled. "We have... haven't we. We'll see what it's doing after supper, we can always drive if we have to."

Thompson helped his wife out of the car and together they hurried into the house.

"I'll go and get supper started; it will only take a few minutes. I don't have much to do tonight to get it ready, and I'm grateful for that after all we've been through," she said, hanging her coat in the hall. "You're sure you don't mind an early supper?"

"No....not a bit."

"Do you find the house a bit damp or is it just me?" she asked, pulling on an apron and tying it about her waist.

"Perhaps a wee bit, now that you mention it. I'll throw some coal on the fire in the front room; it won't take that long to warm the place up. And while I'm at it I'll turn on the electric heater in the kitchen."

"Willie, before you go."

"What is it love?"

"Ooh, it just now crossed my mind that we'd better talk to Aggie."

"Aye, we should do that before we do anything else."

"I do hope she's home. I don't want her hearing about this terrible thing from anyone else. If she does she's bound to think the worst."

"Aye...aye, you're right. I'll go and call her now." He walked to the bottom of the stairs and called his daughter, but there was no answer.

"Aggie, are you up there?" he called a second time.

Thinking she might have closed her bedroom door or perhaps fallen asleep, he climbed the stairs to see if she was in her room.

"There's no sign of her Mary. She must have gone out after all," he called from the top of the stairs.

"Oh dear... well let's hope she won't be long."

"I'm sure she'll be back any minute. She can't have gone far and while we're waiting I'll go ahead and start the fire."

"That would be nice."

"You'll know where I am if you need me."

She turned back towards the kitchen then quickly retraced her steps to where her husband was bent over the fireplace. "Willie, I think I'll try and reach Bertie before I start the supper and I'll write Podraic and get it in the post first thing in the morning. They will want to know right away and I'd feel better if I got word to them as soon as possible."

"Aye love, that would be wise."

Thompson sat in silence and wondered how they were going to manage. He had offered to help with supper, but his wife told him she could manage on her own and although she hadn't said it in so many words he knew she too felt the need to be by herself. Molly would recover, she had to, he told himself, and so would little Tommy. Dr. Kennedy had told them as much, but he did say it would take time and it was too early to tell if they would suffer any permanent disability. The doctor had also told them it might be necessary to send them both to Belfast as soon as they were well enough. Of the two, Molly's condition appeared to be the more serious. He thought about both of them and about what had happened. His father's words about how important a man's family is took on a whole new meaning. The family would pull together; he would see to that, and when the worst was behind them, they would be the stronger for it. His thoughts turned to his other children, to his oldest son in particular. He wondered how soon he would leave for Africa, and what he would find there when he arrived, and how long it might be before he saw him again. He loved him and it was time he told him that himself, perhaps now more than ever.

He felt his wife's hand lightly caress his shoulder. "Darling, supper's on the table," she whispered, kissing him lightly on the forehead.

"Thanks love," he replied, reaching back to touch her hand. "Were you able to get a hold of Bertie?" he asked hopefully.

"Yes, I was, just as he was leaving the flat. He's going to call back tomorrow night to see how they are, and as you can well imagine, he's terribly upset."

"Well, that's about all we can do for now."

"I know that, but I wish I was able to speak to Podraic. It's a pity he's so far away." She stood for a moment resting her hand on his shoulder. "Would you like to have your supper in here rather than at the kitchen table?"

"No, I'll take it in the kitchen."

"You're sure?"

"Aye...."

"Well, come on then, have it while it's hot."

He pulled himself up and walked behind her into the kitchen. She had prepared a bowl of hot broth and a plate of freshly sliced chicken sandwiches garnished with tomatoes and lettuce.

"That's very tasty," he said, taking another spoonful of broth.

"I'm glad you're enjoying it."

"A good broth's hard to beat."

"It is, and the nice thing about it, it doesn't take long to heat up once it's made."

"Aren't you having any?"

"No... I'm not that hungry, but I will have a sandwich and a small salad with my tea....it's almost steeped."

"Mary, I wish you'd have more than that."

"No, that'll be enough. For to tell you the truth, my heart's not in it. Willie, if you don't mind, I thought we might drop into the chapel before we go back to the hospital or if you like we could do it on the way home."

"Well...why don't you?"

"Will you come with me? It would mean a lot to me if we could go together and we needn't be there that long, I promise. It's just that I would feel so much better if we did. God knows we're going to need all the help we can get."

"Aye, I'll go."

"Oh, darling, I am pleased. Would you like your tea now?" she asked, getting up from the table and lifting the teapot from the stove.

"Please."

"Aggie will come too."

"Well, you can ask her when she gets here."

"Oh, I will... I'm surprised she's not back by now."

"Dear, I wouldn't worry. She must have finished her work and gone out sometime after we left. And if she did she would be in no rush to come home for she would expect us to be at Molly's for most of the day."

"I suppose you're right."

"You know I am."

"All the same, I'd feel more content if she was home."

"I know that, but I'm sure she won't be much longer."

They finished the rest of their meal in silence.

"Mary, why don't you have your tea in the front room, that way you can stretch out and give yourself a bit of a rest, maybe even catch a wee nap before we have to leave again."

"Aye, maybe I will."

"You look worn out, darling."

"I am..."

"Here, give me your cup."

"Just a drop, then."

176

Thompson poured a little hot tea into his wife's cup and walked with her into the living room. He handed her the cup and saucer and sat down in the other chair in front of the fireplace. For several minutes they sat quietly watching the fire as they had done the night before.

"I'm not sure I want the tea, after all."

"Well, then... why don't you put your head back?"

"Yes... yes, I think I will," she said wearily, carefully handing him her cup and saucer.

"Would you prefer to go upstairs?"

"No, it's nice by the fire."

"Well lie back, then, and take the good of it."

She slipped off her shoes and sank down into the chair. "Don't let me sleep too long...."

"I won't, love. I promise."

"You're a good man Willie Thompson."

Thompson thought he heard the front door open, but he wasn't sure. He must have dozed off too. He glanced up at the Waterford crystal clock on the mantle and realized he had been asleep for a good half an hour. He heard Aggie in the hallway and waited for her to come into the room. She hadn't said anything about going out when they left this morning and he was glad she was finally home.

"Hello Daddy."

"Sssh, darling, your mother's asleep."

"You're home early."

"Aye.... I'm afraid we are."

"What's wrong?"

He got up and walked quietly into the kitchen. Aggie followed him and stood with her back to the sink holding herself in her arms. There was something wrong, she could tell by the look on her father's face and it frightened her.

"What is it, Daddy? Is there something wrong with mommy?"

"No... no, your mother's fine, Aggie.

177

"What is it, then?"

"It's Molly....and the baby. They're both in the hospital."

"Oh, daddy, what's happened to them? Please tell me it's not something bad."

"I'm afraid it is."

"Ooh mammy dear. Daddy tell me they're going to be alright."

He paused for a moment trying to decide what he was going to say and just how much he should tell her.

"Oh, please Daddy...please say they're alright."

"They're badly hurt, but as far as we know they're both going to be alright."

She sat down beside her father at the table and tearfully listened while he told her everything that had happened. When he finished she wiped her eyes and hugged him.

"Oh, Daddy, they really will be alright... won't they?"

"I hope so...but we'll just have to wait and see how they do."

"Our Molly, she'll beat it, you'll see..."

"I believe she will, darling, but she's going to need our help."

"Why would anyone do such a horrible thing?"

"I wish I knew Aggie."

"I hate them, I do... I hate them."

"Hush now, darling."

"I hate them, daddy."

Thompson nodded. "Aye love...I know."

"Ooh.... poor Molly!"

He felt his anger returning and quickly turned towards the window so that she would not see his face. "Now, go on and get yourself dried off before your mother sees you. And change those wet clothes before you catch your death of cold."

The rain settled in for the evening, as he knew it would. It wasn't a heavy rain, like the rain of the previous night, but a soft steady drizzle, the kind of rain that soaked everything it touched. The town was almost deserted. Only a few people scurried along the darkened streets hugging the fronts of buildings for whatever shelter they could find as they made their way to wherever it was they were going. Thompson slipped the package of Gallaghers into his overcoat pocket, climbed back into the car and drove the short distance back to Nursery Avenue. A short time earlier he had dropped his wife and daughter off at the house on the way from the chapel and driven into the town to buy cigarettes. It wasn't that he really needed them, but they provided the excuse he needed to be by himself, even if only for a short time. Seeing Molly for the second time upset him all over again, and the wee fellow, who was coming along so well a few hours earlier, now seemed to have taken a turn for the worst. He felt numb inside and began to wonder if he himself was partly to blame for what had happened. Perhaps he should have been more insistent that Molly return to Coleraine after her husband went to England and never bothered to return. For a time they both had difficulty trying to understand why she would want to remain on her own in Ballycastle after her husband deserted her. And to add to their distress, the husband had refused to provide financial support for his wife and infant son. That angered him more than anything else for he couldn't understand how a father could walk out on his own son and accept no responsibility for the child's welfare. He had offered to help find her a house in Coleraine, but she had refused. Moving back to the town was not something she wanted to do, and besides, she wasn't about to give up her job, especially now. He wondered too had they gone to Ballycastle on the Saturday instead of the Sunday if it would have made a difference. Or for that matter, had he thought about it earlier in the week, he could easily have brought them to Coleraine for the weekend and driven them home on Sunday afternoon as he had done on other occasions.

He pulled the car over to the side of the road and sat for a few minutes reflecting on what he might have done differently. In the end he was prepared to acknowledge there was probably nothing he could have done to avert this terrible thing, and yet in his heart a lingering sense of guilt remained.

Weeping, he closed his eyes and for the first time in many years offered up a silent, earnest prayer to the God he hardly knew. Alone in the car, he remembered kneeling as a boy at morning prayer, barely able to see over the top of the pew in front of him, and in his hand a Church of Ireland hymn book.

The small boy rose to sing as the sound of the organ filled that ancient place.....

Upon the Cross of Jesus
Mine eyes by faith can see
The very dying form of One
Who suffered there for me;
And from my smitten heart with tears
Two wonders I confess,
The wonder of his glorious love,
And my own worthlessness.

Chapter Sixteen

Father Nolan poked the fire back to life and poured himself a small whiskey, the second since arriving home a few hours ago. Mrs Cassidy had seen to it that he had taken a good supper and mercifully left him alone to enjoy it in peace. On the way back from Ballymena it had started to rain and from the look of the sky he was certain it was likely to rain most of the night. He turned from the window and made his way across the room to his favourite chair in front of the fire. How would he feel, he wondered, when the time finally came to leave this place, a place where he had spent much of his life? Cushendall had become his home and over the years he had grown to love the town and the people who inhabited it. The events of the past few hours had shaken him badly and caused him to reflect again on his own pastoral ministry. Perhaps his old mentor was right after all when he once told him that he had spent too much time making people happy and not enough time making people good. At the time, it struck him as an odd thing for a priest to say. Now he understood and he wondered if he too had made the same mistake in caring for the flock of Christ entrusted to his care.

Mrs Cassidy came into the room, gathered up the supper plate and walked silently back to the kitchen leaving him alone to finish his whiskey. A few minutes later she returned with a cup of hot tea and sat it down on the small table beside his chair. She had been remarkably quiet all evening. He had noticed it earlier when he first returned from Ballymena, but had wisely chosen to let sleeping dogs lie, especially this one. After what he'd been through earlier in the day he was entitled to a few hours peace and quiet. And with the likes of Mrs. Cassidy, he knew from past experience, it wasn't likely to last long. All the same, she wasn't herself and he began to wonder if there was something seriously wrong. The long ash from his cigarette dropped onto his cassock and out of habit he flicked it to the floor with his finger. Luckily, she hadn't noticed or his peace would have been short lived.

"Are you feeling alright, Mrs Cassidy?"

"Oh, I'm well enough."

"You've hardly said a word all night."

"Ooh, you noticed, did you?"

"Of course I noticed.... not that I'm complaining, mind you."

"No, I don't suppose you are."

"It's not like you to be that quiet."

"Aye, well..."

"Is there something wrong?"

"Aye, maybe so..."

"Well, out with it, woman."

"Some things are best left unsaid, Father."

"Good God, woman, if there's something wrong spit it out. I've never known you to bite your tongue before."

"I've never had cause until now."

"Well, suit yourself. I've better things to do than argue with a contrary oull woman."

"Would you listen to yourself?"

"I'd sooner do that, than listen to the likes of you."

"Aye, well, you can say what you like...but I'll tell you one thing Father....you won't see the likes of me cosying up to the police."

"Ooh, so that's it."

"As if you didn't know."

"Know...know what, for God's sake?"

"God help me, I never thought I'd see the day... and you one of us. You ought to be ashamed of yourself."

"Mind your tongue... we'll have none of that."

"I'll do no such thing."

"Good God, woman, have you lost your mind?"

"Oh.... there's a good one. No...there's nothing wrong with my mind for I haven't forgotten what side I'm on. I'm not sure I can say the same for you, God forgive me for saying it."

"That's it, then."

"Aye," she said coldly.

She picked up the few dishes that were left and turned to leave the room.

"Mrs Cassidy...for God's sake woman, haven't you heard?" he shouted after her.

"Oh, I've heard. Sure the whole town's talking about it."

Father Nolan shook his head. "I suppose they are and God help me, why am I not surprised?" he asked wearily.

"Oh they are... and I'll tell you something else... I wouldn't give the RUC the time of day. They're a bad rotten crowd make no mistake about it. And you ought to have nothing to do with them. Let them do their own dirty work...the dirty rascals."

"I think you've said enough."

"Oh, I'm sure you do, but I'll say my piece if it's all the same to you. And I'll tell you something else while I'm at it... I'm not the only one in Cushendall who thinks it. There are others in the parish who feel the same way."

"Is that a fact?"

"Aye... it is."

"I see...."

"I'm not sure that you do. You of all people should understand that feelings run deep in this part of the country. We're not used to seeing our priest in the company of the police."

"My God, woman, we're talking about murder....the murder of innocent people, not some foolish escapade by a bunch of bloody halfwits out to destroy a bit of property."

"Oh, are we now? Well, it's not the first time innocent people have died in Ireland... and I hardly think it'll be the last," she said bitterly, turning again towards the kitchen.

"Then, God help us all, Mrs Cassidy."

"Oh, I'm sure he will, Father....it's his own he looks after."

"Och, away with you. Go on, go home out of my sight and ask God to forgive you....away with you now before I say something I might regret."

"Well, I meant no harm."

"Oh didn't you now?"

"Will you be wanting anything else?" she asked hesitantly.

"Oh, I hardly think so, Mrs Cassidy."

"I'm away then."

He ignored her.

She walked hurriedly out of the room leaving him alone with his anger. He finished the whiskey and set the empty glass on the table. For a moment he considered refilling the glass, but decided against it. His mood had changed.

"Damn that woman!"

To his relief he heard the front door slam behind her and not a minute too soon for his liking. He thought again about what she had just said and the terrible hatred in her voice when she said it. He knew he had done the right thing, but he didn't doubt for a minute there were others in the parish who believed like Mrs Cassidy that their priest had no business helping the RUC under any circumstances. A few might even secretly accuse him of betraying his own kind. The thought hadn't entered his mind when he agreed earlier in the day to accompany the police to

Ballymena. But now he came to the painful realization that his act of compassion would almost certainly be misunderstood by his own people; a small number might even stop coming altogether. Cushendall was a small place and he knew how quickly news of his involvement with the police would spread throughout the parish. There was nothing else he could have done he told himself and he would now have to live with the consequences, however unpleasant or painful they might be. For his part, he would do what he could to restore their confidence and the rest he would leave to God. Sadly he realized that for some there would be no possibility of reconciliation, no acknowledgement at all that he had only done what any other responsible person would have done if placed in the same situation. At that moment he remembered what Inspector Hamill had said about the need for decent people to speak out if this madness was going to stop.

Father Nolan waited for his anger to subside before rising to his feet and pulling on his winter coat. Outside the fog and drizzle had reduced visibility to a few hundred yards and by the look of things it would only get worse as the night wore on. Already a cold moist breeze was blowing in from the sea. With a heavy heart he crossed the lawn and opened the oak door that led directly into the sanctuary. The chapel was virtually empty. Only a handful of parishioners, mostly elderly women, knelt in silent prayer clutching their rosaries in their hands. The sweet familiar fragrance of incense still hung in the damp night air. The old priest made the sign of the cross and falling to his knees made his Act of Contrition.

O my God, I am heartily sorry for having offended Thee, and I detest all my sins, because I dread the loss of Heaven and the pains of Hell, but most of all because they offend Thee, my God, who art all-good and deserving of all my love...

Again he sought God's forgiveness as he brought to mind the things he had done and the things he had left undone. He prayed for tolerance and understanding among the people he had been called to love and serve. With wonder he gazed upon the crucified Christ certain in the knowledge that, unworthy though he was and however difficult the months ahead might be, nothing in heaven or on earth could separate him from the love of God in Christ Jesus. And bowing in adoration he cast his burden at the feet of the merciful Christ. "Oh, what manner of love is this that the Father has bestowed upon us," he whispered, as he raised his weary old eyes to behold the Blessed Virgin.

Lord, have mercy.
Christ, have mercy....
Holy Mary, Mother of God, pray for us....

Chapter Seventeen

They're on to us, or they bloody well soon will be, Tommy McCann shouted at the woman, as he came scurrying through the door into the kitchen. He had just driven into the yard in the Riley.

"Oh for God's sake, man, get a hold of yourself," Angela said, startled by McCann's abrupt and unexpected outburst.

"I'm telling you, they're on to us."

"Who's on to us?"

"Who the bloody hell do you think? The police, who else? And by now, I would think half the British Army."

"God man, are you sure?"

"Oh, I'm bloody sure, alright. I've just heard from our man in Cushendall. It seems a local man found the lorry early this morning and reported it to the RUC."

"Where?"

"On the coast road."

"Those stupid bloody fools! All they had to do was drive it to the edge of the cliffs at Runabay Head and push it into the sea. It was simple enough."

"Oh, it was supposed to be."

"Christ, what are you saying?"

"I'm saying they never got a chance."

"But what could possibly have gone wrong?"

"I don't know and our man doesn't know either. When I asked him, all he could tell me is that the wreck was found lying upside down among the rocks just off the road. The weather was bad on the coast road last night and for all we know they may have been driving too bloody fast. That's a bad stretch of road at the best of times. There's no other explanation."

"Of all the times to have a bloody accident."

"Aye... you can say that again."

"But how can you be so certain they're on to us? A wrecked lorry won't tell them much even if they link it to the bombing in Ballycastle."

"Young Draper, that's how. Our man says the police have him and worse, he's gone and seen a priest and God only knows what he's told him. I always said he never seemed to be able to make up his mind if he was really one of us and that's the worst bloody kind to have to rely on when things go wrong."

"Damn him!" Her eyes flashed in anger at the sudden realization that McCann might be right after all. "Damn that treacherous little bastard."

"Aye, well, he's gone and done it, or so our man says, and at this point I have no reason to doubt him. For all I know, the little prick may have fingered the lot of us."

"Christ...."

"I can't swear to it, mind you, but I'm not waiting around here to find out."

"What about the other one...the driver?"

"He's dead." McCann snapped back.

"Well, at least we won't have to worry about him talking to the police, or anyone else for that matter."

McCann watched her walk to the kitchen table, reach for her

purse and calmly light a cigarette. Her anger, which was so evident just moments earlier, was suddenly gone. She slid the package of cigarettes across the table. "Here, help yourself, you look as if you could use one."

He shook his head.

"Tommy, can we get to him?" she asked blowing a small cloud of smoke across the room in his direction.

Jesus, he thought, that's one cool bitch. It's as if she was asking him what the weather will be like tomorrow morning.

"Well?"

"Who, for God's sake?"

"Draper...who else?"

"Not too bloody likely, unless you intend to ambush the police and that would be bloody madness after what happened last night. The countryside will be crawling with them. No. If you want my advice you'll forget about Draper. There's not a damned thing we can do about him. We've more urgent things to take care of right now."

"And the priest....?"

"Jesus woman, what are you thinking?" She was about to say something else, but McCann cut her off abruptly. "The Humber... it will have to be driven to Belfast tonight," he said, shaking his head in disbelief.

"That's too risky."

"Aye, it's risky to be sure, but what other choice do we have. My guess is if we wait and leave it until tomorrow morning it may be too late. No... my mind's made up....it will have to be tonight. We can't risk losing the arms' shipment. Not now...it's cost too bloody much already."

"You're probably right...."

"I know I am. I'll drive it into the city tonight and the sooner I leave the better."

"I still think it's risky to be on the road at this time of the night."

"Aye, well, unless you have a better plan it's the only option open to us. It's a bit late now to be thinking about doing anything else. And let's face it, we have no way of knowing how much the police have been told or for that matter what they've managed to piece together. For all we know they may already know who we are, and I for one don't intend to sit on my arse waiting to find out. And if you're smart you won't be long after me."

"Oh, I won't... I'll leave as soon as I see to this place."

"Well, I would be quick about it. They may even know about this place."

He grabbed his heavy overcoat and walked quickly into the yard, not bothering to look back or close the door behind him. A few minutes later, the Humber roared into life. Cautiously, he eased her out of the shed and coached the big car into the long narrow lane that would take him onto the secondary road skirting the town of Cushendun. Once he reached the main road he was confident he would be able to make better time, and with luck might be in Belfast within the hour. But the risk of detection, he knew, would be significantly greater.

Chapter Eighteen

Inspector Hamill put down the phone and wearily pushed his chair away from the large wooden desk where he had been working for the better part of the evening. Earlier, before leaving Ballymena, he had called his wife and told her not to expect him for supper. She was used to it by now, but he knew she would keep his supper in the oven just the same, hoping he would arrive home before it was ruined. He seldom did and tonight would be no exception. He stood up and walked to the window. It was raining again and the wind, which had risen earlier in the evening, carried a bank of fog into Belfast Lough. From where he stood, he could see the lights of the Albert Street Bridge and the stream of headlights moving slowly along the Sydenham Road on the other side of the harbour. In the distance he could hear the muted clanging of an ambulance. Belfast looked peaceful enough, but he knew better.

"Excuse me sir, but I thought you would want to know..."

He turned from the window and nodded to the police officer standing by the door. "Och... come on in sergeant."

"Sir, I have just been informed a tactical squad has been

dispatched to Cushendun."

"What time did they leave?"

"Oh I think almost an hour ago...."

"Good, then we won't have to wait long, will we?"

"No....I shouldn't think so, sir."

Inspector Hamill rubbed both eyes with his hands, yawned, and turned back towards the window. For a short time, he stood staring down at the wet street four storeys below. A double decker bus groaned to a halt and a handful of people hastily folded their umbrellas and scrambled up onto the back of the bus. As he watched, the bus pulled away from the kerb and quickly disappeared in the rain and fog that was now beginning to engulf the city. For a moment he wished he too had boarded the bus and gone home. It had been a long exhausting day and given the events of the past few hours, there was no reason to believe it would be over anytime soon. At that moment he would have given anything for a shower and a clean shirt. A hot bath would have suited his mood even better, but that wasn't about to happen either. His thoughts turned to his wife. Occasionally they used to take baths together when they were first married. He couldn't remember why they'd stopped other than the fact that at some point the novelty just wore off. But whatever the reason, they never seemed to bother with that sort of thing anymore and their love making was sporadic at best. His wife, he thought, seemed less interested than he was, but to be fair he wasn't really sure. The street below was deserted now and as he stared into the darkness he thought again of Father Nolan and what the priest had told him. Turning from the window he wondered how they would manage if it turned out that Ballycastle was only the beginning of something far more terrible.

"Did you say something, Inspector?"

"Oh, I was just thinking, sergeant. Wondering if what the lad told the old priest is correct." He paused, reflecting for a brief moment on what he had just said. "I hope not. Things are difficult enough for us these days without having to cope with this kind of violence in other parts of the province. The riots that broke out in Derry and Belfast were worse than anyone expected and as it turned out, far more than we could handle without the help of the British Army."

"But what if he's right?"

"I'm not sure I can answer that...but I'll tell you this, we're ill prepared to deal with the sort of thing that happened in Ballycastle last night. For one thing, there's really no way of knowing who or what will be targeted next. That's the worst kind of trouble for the police to have to deal with. But what worries me even more, sergeant, is the possibility the IRA will now deliberately target civilians. That's something we've not had to deal with before. And if what we've been told turns out to be the case, we can only hope that ordinary people themselves will reach a point where they demand an end to sectarian violence once and for all. Perhaps then this country of ours will have a chance for peace."

The sergeant nodded his head solemnly.

"Aye... you would hope so."

"When it happens, sergeant, don't be surprised that it's the women who speak out first. They are the ones left to bury their sons and their husbands."

"That's true."

"Only time will tell, sergeant."

"Aye, that's true too. Will there be anything else, sir?"

"No....no, that's all. Just pull the door behind you like a good fellow. I might try to put my head down for a few minutes."

The sergeant started back towards the door.

"Oh...there is one more thing."

"What's that, sir?"

"It's a long shot, I know, but have we had any word from Liverpool yet?"

"No....not a thing."

"Hmm...."

"The Chief Constable's office was contacted this afternoon, right after you called from the hospital in Ballymena."

"That's that, then."

"I'm afraid so...at least for the moment."

"All the same, I was hoping we might have heard something by now."

"Aye, and to be truthful I was hoping the same thing. I think we all were. Still, it's early, sir. I think the important thing is that at our end we lost no time in giving them the information we had. It's their show across the water now."

The Inspector looked wearily at his wrist watch; it was almost half past ten. "Yes....yes, I suppose you're right," he said, with a dry smile, not bothering to look up as the sergeant closed the door behind him.

He crossed the room and again sat down behind the desk he had left a few minutes earlier. As the evening wore on it began to rain heavier. He hadn't noticed it before, but now he could hear the rain and wind pelting the window overlooking the street. It was another wet, dreary night in Belfast. "After awhile you'll get used to the weather and the sombre mood of the place in winter; you'll see." That's what they'd told him when he first arrived in the city. And they were right. For in time, he came to accept the changing face of a city that embraced the onslaught of winter with stoic indifference. The weather outside suited his mood. It was a good night for brooding, for sorting things out. A good night to put the pieces of the puzzle together and now, thanks to Father Nolan they were beginning to come together rather quickly. But he had been a policeman too long to assume that things would fall into place without some unforeseen difficulty. And yet, sometimes you were fortunate enough to have the right information at the right time and that was often the difference between success and failure. He hoped that was the case in this instance. By now the heavily armed tactical squad should be approaching Cushendun and with luck they would not have to wait much longer to learn the outcome. Scotland Yard had also been notified that Meagher had travelled on the overnight ferry to Liverpool the night before. If only they'd known sooner, he thought, Meagher might have been arrested as he stepped off the boat. Now, that seemed a remote possibility. The trouble was a man could get lost quickly in a city the size of Liverpool, especially with the help of friends, and the IRA had plenty of them in Liverpool. The possibility that Meagher may have again slipped through their fingers angered him, but the truth was there was nothing he could do about it now, however much he might have wished it otherwise. His head fell back on the chair and a few minutes later he was sound asleep.

"Inspector....sir, wake up."

"What....what...good God man what is it? And what time is it?"

"Sir, it's after eleven....and sir... we have them....we have the bastards. The tactical squad spotted the hearse just as it was turning onto the main road. The driver apparently tried to make a run for it and took a bullet for his trouble...and the woman... they arrested just as she was preparing to leave. She apparently tried to run one of our officers down as she left the yard."

"Well....that's that then....this time we had a bit of luck after all."

The inspector rose and slowly walked back to the window overlooking the street without saying anything else. He was grateful that things had gone so well, but as he stood staring into the darkness he wondered if they would be so lucky the next time, for there was no doubt at all in his mind there would be a next time.

Chapter Nineteen

Thompson thought he heard Mary's voice as she walked through the back door into the kitchen.

"What....what's that, love?"

"I said, you're very quiet."

"I suppose I am."

"You've hardly spoken a word since you came in and you haven't touched a bit of toast."

Thompson looked at his wife and then at the two slices of toast sitting on his plate. "No, I haven't, have I?" he said, reaching for the toast that was now quite cold.

"Oh leave it. I'll make you another."

"Aye, well, that'll do. I'm afraid the day's taken more out of me than I'm prepared to admit, even to myself."

"Oh don't I know it....God knows I feel the same way. The truth is I'm worried sick about them and now more than ever after seeing them again tonight. I know it could be worse, but somehow that's little comfort when I see the way they are."

"I know...I know that, but it could have been a lot worse. And sure earlier this afternoon we thought it was. They're both alive and that's what matters, you said so yourself."

Mary nodded. "Aye, God help me I did, didn't I."

"And you meant it too...."

"I did," she said, wiping her eyes with the corner of her apron. "I shouldn't have said that...."

"Oh, don't be too hard on yourself."

She lifted the teapot and filled his cup with hot tea. "There now, drink it while it's hot, you'll get the good of it that way and your toast will be up in a minute," she said, trying to put what she had just said behind her.

He buttered the warm toast and cut himself a small piece of cheddar cheese. He always had his toast and tea before going to bed; it had become a habit and it never occurred to him that he might be better off without it.

Mary poured herself a small cup and pulled her chair closer to her husband. "There, that will do me, I'm not feeling much like anything tonight," she said, as she reached over and lightly stroked the back of his hand. "I don't think there's much else we can do tonight...."

"No, I don't suppose there is."

"We'll have to wait and see how they are in the morning. Let's hope and pray they'll be alright."

"Aye...."

"Willie, did you hear me, love?"

"I'm sorry, my mind just wandered for a moment."

"I thought as much, I could tell by the look on your face you weren't listening. I said we need to pray for them... it will help, I know it will."

Thompson glanced down at the small hand resting on his. "We'll do that too," he said softly. It was what she needed to hear at that moment and she was right about them needing all the help they could get. If only Molly had stayed at home, he thought, or perhaps walked back another way it might have turned out differently. But the bitter truth was there was no sense to any of it and dwelling on what might have happened would change absolutely nothing.

She raised her hand and gently touched the small Celtic cross hanging about her neck.

"Mary do you remember when we were first married?"

"Of course I do," she said, squeezing his hand, "what a silly thing to say as if I could ever forget something like that."

"No....I don't mean that. I mean the time we went looking for a flat in Belfast. For some reason I was thinking about that when you were out in the yard looking after the dog, and again, just now, when you held your wee cross."

"It's the one you bought me soon after we were married."

"Aye it is, but do you remember the woman in Belfast who owned the flat?"

"Yes. Yes I think I do, now that you mention it."

"You thought it was a lovely flat."

"We both did as I recall."

"Aye, we did."

"I remember thinking how lucky we were to have found it and how kind the old woman was when we first met her. I recall her saying we were just the sort of young couple she was hoping to find, and how pleased she was when we agreed to rent it."

"She wasn't that old."

"No, I don't suppose she was, but at the time, she seemed old to us."

"I suppose...."

"She seemed such a kind person."

"I thought so too."

Mary lowered her eyes, and brushed an imaginary piece of lint from her skirt. "I think it was the way she said it, as much as anything. That's what hurt me the most. I remember the look on her face when we got up to leave and she noticed the cross hanging around my neck. That's when she asked me if I was Catholic, by any chance. When I told her I was, she said she was sorry, but she couldn't possibly rent us the flat. Just like that.... I can't recall now whether I felt sorrier for her or for myself.

Perhaps I felt sorry for both of us."

"Well, it was you I felt sorry for."

Mary got up from the table and started to clear away the dishes. "I thought that kind of thing was behind us; now I'm not so sure," she said, gazing into the darkness beyond the kitchen window.

Thompson sat for a few moments quietly milling over in his mind what she had just said. They had only lived in Belfast for the year and it was long enough. Coleraine was a quiet town and a decent place to live and raise a family. He had been born and raised in the borough and never had any real desire to leave it, even when work was scarce and more plentiful elsewhere. For the most part, people were tolerant too and that was something that could not be said for a lot of other places in Northern Ireland. Only on the twelfth of July were sectarian lines drawn in the town, mostly in working class neighbourhoods where streets were painted in the traditional orange and purple to commemorate King Billy's victory at the battle of the Boyne. But it was a short lived affair, and the next day Catholics and Protestants alike went back to work and got on with their lives with little or no animosity. Only the frightening sound of the lambeg drum lingered on to haunt the minds of young children, long after the rain had washed the bright orange and purple paint from the streets. As did the awful sight of men staggering under the weight of those enormous drums, their eyes puffed and red from drink and their hands raw and bleeding from pounding the drums with large sticks that looked like bulrushes.

"Still, I must admit, we haven't had much trouble in Coleraine," Mary added, still gazing into the darkness.

"No... nothing of any account."

"We've been very fortunate, and may it please God to keep it that way," she said earnestly, as she finished wiping the table with a damp cloth and putting the last of the dishes in the sink.

"You're coming to bed?"

"In a little while, love."

"Och, Mary dear, would you leave it?"

"I won't be long, I promise."

"Aye well, suit yourself."

"I'll only be a minute, you'll see."

He shook his head. "You'll never change, will you?"

"No, I don't suppose I will. It's just that I like to leave things ready for the morning and you know how I feel about tidying up the kitchen after a meal. It's what we always did when I was growing up."

Mary placed the butter and cheese in the larder and walked back to the sink. Rinsing the dishcloth in hot water she quickly finished the dishes and stacked them neatly in the drying rack beside the sink. "There, that's done, all that's left to do is dry them and put them away," she said, smiling at her husband. "I won't be much longer. Then, if you don't mind, I would just like to sit down for a minute or two. I'm not myself tonight and God knows it's no wonder after what we've been through."

A few minutes later she sat down at the kitchen table and with her elbows resting on the table buried her face in her hands.

"Willie..."

"What is it love?"

"Do you ever get tired?"

"Of course, I do."

"No...I mean, really tired."

"Ooh, sometimes, sure we all do. It's a common enough complaint, but most of us manage to bounce back after a good night's sleep. Mind you, it seems to take a little longer as you get older."

"I suppose so, but lately it just seems a little more difficult."

"It's not like you to talk like that."

"No I know. Maybe I'm just beginning to feel my age."

"Och, catch yourself on. Sure, you're still a young woman."

"It's nice you think so."

"Well, I do, come on now it's time you went to bed."

"Willie, I'm so afraid, not just for Molly and Tommy, God love them, but for all of us. I've been thinking all day that if something like that could happen in a quiet town like Ballycastle, it could happen anywhere, even right here in Coleraine. It's frightening when you allow yourself to think about it. I can't help thinking too of the families that are left with a heavy heart, tonight."

"Aye... that's the worst part of it. Still I find it hard to believe it would happen here. Coleraine has always been such a peaceful place; sure it's one of the reasons we've been so content here."

"But you can't really be sure."

"No I can't, I don't suppose anyone can."

Mary got to her feet and stood by the kitchen window. A tear rolled down one cheek and then the other. "Oh dear God, I need to make some sense out of this terrible day. Please tell me it will be alright."

Thompson took his wife in his arms. He kissed her gently on the forehead and then on her lips.

"Hold me closer darling," she whispered, trying to hold back her tears. She bit her lower lip and buried her head in his shoulder.

"There...let it go, let it all out, love."

"Oh, my poor darling, Molly."

"There, now..."

He held her until her sobbing stopped.

"I love you, Willie," she said, wiping her eyes with her hand.

"I know, darling."

"I've always loved you."

"Aye, I know that too."

"I want to go to bed now," she said softly. "I need you to hold me."

He took her hand and led her up the stairs to the privacy of their own bedroom. It had always been a special place, a kind of sanctuary where they shut the door on the world outside, a place where they found each other even when things were bad between them. It was a place where she gave herself willingly to the man she loved more than anything else in the world. Not more than God and the Blessed Virgin, she told herself often, but in her heart she knew the truth. He was all she'd ever wanted. His hand found her and she opened herself to him. They held each other as he slipped easily into her in the practised way a man does with a woman familiar to him. She arched her back and pushed her lower body against him, gently at first, then harder as his movements quickened and became more urgent. Afterwards, they lay where they were, enjoying the warmth that lingered about them.

"Ooh, that was lovely!"

"Aye..." He said, his breathing still laboured from their lovemaking.

"Are you alright, love?"

"Oh, of course I am. It's just that I'm not as young as I once was."

"Well, you'd never know it." She couldn't see his face in the dark, but she was sure he was smiling.

He felt her move again beneath him and he wished, just for once, that he was young and not old.

"We'd better get up and wash."

"No.... no, I'd like us to stay just as we are."

"But, darling..."

"No.... I'll change the sheets in the morning."

"If that's what you want."

"Yes....that's what I want."

They lay together in silence and only when it felt right did they turn to their own side of the bed.

"Goodnight, love."

"Goodnight..."

Half an hour latter Mary heard the clock downstairs strike

eleven o'clock. She hadn't fallen asleep and in her head she counted out all eleven chimes. The house fell silent again. She rolled over towards her husband and put her arm around him.

"Sweetheart."

"What is it?"

"Are you asleep?"

"No."

"Oh, I hope I didn't wake you."

"No....I was just lying here, thinking."

"What about?"

"Ooh, about you and the children."

"Willie, I wish they were closer."

"Aye, me too." He reached out and put his arm gently around her soft slender waist, moving his hand slowly upward until he felt the roundness of her breast. "You're still a lovely woman, Mary."

"You always say that when you've had your way with me."

"Well, you are."

She had no reason to doubt him. Even when she was carrying each of their four children and felt as big as a house and just as awkward, he never failed to notice her. And once when she was carrying Aggie, she overheard Podraic telling his brother that their mammy looked like a pear with two sticks for legs. She had laughed at the pair of them. But a short time later she ran to her bedroom and cried. He found her there and loved her as he had tonight, telling her supper could wait.... and it did.

"We've had a good life, Willie.... haven't we?"

"Better than most, I reckon."

"I remember you telling me about the woman who lived in Park Street...I can't remember her name."

"Mrs Brown...."

"Yes, that's her."

"She was around my mother's age."

"I remember you telling me she'd only been out of the town

204

once in her whole life."

"Aye, that's true enough, the day she was married. After the wedding they took the bus and travelled to Portrush for a day's outing by the seaside. And that same evening she came home with her new husband to the house in Park Street where her mother lived and never left the town again. She lived in that same house all her life and raised a big family there too. My father also told me that she only left the street to shop for groceries and whatever else she needed or to attend the christening and confirmation of their children at Saint Patrick's Church, which was just around the corner. The park was at the bottom of the street so she had all she needed right on her own doorstep. I'm not even sure she even ventured over the Bann."

"Somehow, it seems so sad."

"You might say that, but I suppose it's all in the way you look at things."

"I don't doubt it....but still, to think she could spend her whole life in one small part of the town doesn't seem right somehow."

"Aye, well, a lot of women did, even when I was growing up."

"I suppose...."

"That's not to say the Mrs Browns of this world weren't happy. They seemed happy enough as far as anyone could tell. Mind you, it was all they ever knew."

Mary touched his hand. "Perhaps it's true what they say, you don't miss what you've never had, but I wonder if she ever wished for something different."

"Well, if she did, she kept it to herself. I think they all did. My mother was the same."

"Maybe she was content enough, then."

"Oh, I suppose in her own way she was. Mind you, that's not to say that sometimes she may have wished for something better. I think most of us do, at one time or another. It may be nothing more than just wanting enough to get by on without the constant worry of trying to make ends meet. Then again, maybe it's more than that, a better life perhaps for themselves and for their children. I often think too, that some people would like to have a second chance, the chance to do things differently."

Outside on the street the wind had picked up carrying the rain across the open bowling green and throwing it gently against the bedroom window. In the distance he thought he heard the faint rumble of thunder, but it was a long way off.

Closing his eyes he saw the small boy standing alone on a deserted stretch of wind swept sand, looking out to sea in search of his own dream. He drifted silently, ghosting across dark, unchartered water into the shadows of his own heart - a voice unheeded, a road not taken, and in the darkest shadow, a dream that lay just beyond his reach. And when he turned again to look at the stretch of sand beyond the small green meadow, the boy was no longer there.

"Willie!"

"What... what is it?"

"I thought you said something."

"Oh.... I was just remembering something." He struggled to keep his eyes from closing.

She felt his hand fall from her side. They were both tired and needed sleep. She thought again of Molly and their grandson and then of the man who loved her.

"Willie."

"What is it love...." he said wearily.

Mary touched his face, then reached over and kissed him softly on the cheek."Thank you...." she said, turning again to her own side of the bed."

"For what?"

"Ooh, for loving me."

Thompson smiled and rolled on his back trying to find a more comfortable position. The new pillow, somehow, didn't feel right; it was too soft and didn't provide enough support for his head. The old one was more to his liking. He moved his head on

206

the pillow and closed his eyes in search of sleep.

He remembered the first time he kissed her.

On the river bank below Bann Bridge, a young woman moved out from the shadow of the building and walked towards him through a shaft of moonlight that filtered down between the branches of two large chestnut trees. "I snuck out earlier, but you weren't here," she whispered. "I thought you weren't coming.... I can only stay a minute." She kissed him softly with her wet open mouth and pressed her eager young body against his. No one had ever kissed him like that before. And her scent, he remembered, was fresh and sweet like the warm night air itself.

Buffalo gals, won't you come out tonight?
Come out tonight, Come out tonight?
Buffalo gals, won't you come out tonight,
And dance by the light of the moon.

Only the soft pelting of rain on the window panes and the shallow breathing of the woman lying beside him stirred the darkness. God knows she'd been a good wife. More than he deserved. But then, he'd known that for a long time.

"Mary...."

There was no reply.

Mary had finally fallen asleep.

Christmas

Coleraine 1969

Chapter Twenty

Overnight a heavy frost transformed the town into an urban landscape of snow like crystals that glistened in the early morning sunlight. It was as close to a white Christmas as Coleraine was ever likely to get, for in Ireland snow was an uncommon occurrence. And on those rare occasions when it suddenly appeared it disappeared just as quickly and was soon forgotten by all but the smallest children who, for a few fleeting hours, played in carefree delight. By mid morning the frost had vanished and the town looked as it always looked in the now bleak light of a December sky. In the streets last minute shoppers scurried from shop to shop looking for that special gift or for something they had forgotten to buy earlier in the week. Others, less fortunate, searched the aisles of Woolworths looking for small inexpensive presents they could afford to bring home to their children so that on Christmas day they would have something more in their stocking than an apple or an orange. Shop windows were decorated with chain links of brightly coloured paper and sprigs of dark green holly and red berries lying on fluffy beds of white cotton wool. On Church

Street one of the larger shops in the town had a Christmas tree in the window decorated with red and blue lights that flashed off and on. And at the base of the tree a model electric train puffing smoke ran around a circular track and disappeared into a tunnel. Outside on the street a small group of young boys watched as the train reappeared and secretly wished that Santa Claus would bring them a train just like the one in the window. And from the loud speakers in the Diamond, Father Murphy's rich baritone voice could be heard above the crowd singing Christmas carols.

On the train from Derry the young priest sat quietly resting his head against the back of the comfortable seat he had selected near the rear of the carriage. For most of the morning his family, and Molly especially, had been on his mind, and the journey gave him the opportunity to reflect on all that had happened as the train rattled and swayed through the Irish countryside. A short time earlier, when the train pulled away from the station in Downhill, he was reminded of the first time he saw the ruined shell of Downhill Castle and the fascination it had always held for him. On his own, he had read a great deal about the history of the castle and the eccentric cleric who built it, a castle that was not really a castle at all but a Bishop's Palace, built by Frederick Hervey, the Fourth Earl of Bristol and Anglican Bishop of Derry in the eighteenth century. And just beyond the palace, the Mussenden Temple stood, perched precariously on the very edge of the cliff top above Downhill, also built by the Earl-Bishop as a wedding present for his niece who had married a wealthy London banker named Daniel Mussenden. As the train entered the tunnel directly below the temple he closed his eyes and remembered longingly the warm days of a summer not so long ago. Setting out early in the morning, he had ridden his bicycle from his home in Coleraine all the way to Downhill. Once there he spent most of the day exploring the mysteries of the castle and the dark narrow pathways that wound through the Black Glen, often wondering how spectacular the palace and gardens must have been in their original state. Occasionally he coasted down the steep hill past the Lion's Gate into the village and onto Benone Strand which lay in the shadow of the towering cliffs that rose above the narrow coastal road, a place he remembered his father talking so much about when he was growing up.

He remembered too his father telling him it was here his grandfather was buried, not far from the Bishop's Gate. Only once had his father taken him to the small ancient cemetery on the other side of the road in search of the unmarked grave. They had walked in from the road along a narrow path only to find a small sheltered patch of land overgrown by knee-high weeds and thorn bushes. At the far end of the clearing, close to where his father thought the grave might be located, a stone wall covered with ivy marked the outer boundary of the cemetery. And on the other side of the clearing a solitary scarlet fuchsia bush in full bloom stood between two weather worn headstones. Together they cleared away as much of the burial ground as they could without really knowing which part of the clearing held the remains of his great grandfather. He had always meant to go back, but he never did. Perhaps before he left this time he and his father could arrange to visit the grave together. Somehow little Tommy's death brought things into focus. Like generations of his family before him, he too had passed from death into life, into the very presence of the eternal God.

As the train neared the railway bridge that crossed the River Bann the young priest, who was sitting on the other side of the carriage, moved quickly across the aisle to view the town that was so much a part of his life. He had not been home for almost a year, and when the train started across the river towards the station he realized how much he had missed his home. He knew too, it would be a long time before he saw it again. The decision to send him to Nigeria had been made. He would sail for Africa early in the new year and if the experience of others was to be relied upon, it would probably be five years before he was able to return to Ireland. Beyond that he had no way of knowing where God's call would take him or where the church might see fit to send him. Some, he knew, had gone and spent the better part of their life on the African Continent. A few, like the priest he would replace, had never returned. But for now he was home and the future he knew would take care of itself. His thoughts turned to his family again and to Molly in particular, and he wondered how she was really coping with all that had happened in her life. The train slowed as it wound its way to the station and minutes later came to a noisy abrupt stop. He pulled his heavy overcoat and suitcase from the overhead rack and eagerly stepped onto the platform. A few yards from where he stood, he saw his father waiting at the station near the open ticket gate that led to the street.

"Welcome home, son."

"Aye, dad.....it's good to be home." They threw their arms around each other and stood in silent embrace.

"Your mother's waiting for you up at the house son," he said, turning his head quickly towards the exit in an effort to hide his tears. "As you might expect, she's as busy as ever making sure everything is just right. Here, son, let me have your case. The car's just outside on the street and with any luck we'll be home in no time. I'll go up the Ballycastle Road; it'll be quicker than trying to go through the town at this time of the day."

"Dad, what about Molly?" the young priest asked anxiously as they reached the car. There was so much he wanted and needed to know about the family, but Molly was foremost in his thoughts and at that moment it was her welfare that concerned him most. He had written her from Rome and in the letter had tried as best he could to say the right things. Now there was so much more he needed to share with her, the kind of things that could only be said when they were alone together, the sort of things a brother needs to say to his sister.

"Och, son, she's doing as well as you might expect considering

214

all that she's been through....and like the rest of us she's managing as best she can. Some days are better than others, of course, but I'm afraid none of them are that good. It's good you're home, Podraic, I'll say that, for she desperately needs to talk to you and so does your mother."

"Dad, I'm sorry I wasn't home for the funeral. It broke my heart when I received your letters, but sadly there was no way I could have made it home and that's bothered me ever since."

"Son, sure you did everything you could. I know that and so does the rest of the family. The truth is it happened so suddenly. Tommy was doing so well for awhile and the doctors at Bannview gave us no reason to believe anything different. At the beginning we were more worried about Molly than the youngster. Of the two, her condition appeared to be the more serious, but in the end it was little Tommy who took a turn for the worst and died just a few days later. The rest you already know from your mother's letters. God knows it was a sad day, and happening as it did so close to Christmas makes it all the harder to deal with. It was a month ago yesterday. Your mother too, is in a bad way and to tell you the truth I don't know what to say to her any more. And that's something I've never had trouble with before. You know how devout a Catholic she is. She was so certain her prayers would be answered and I think she's struggling with that too. Maybe you'll be able to help her see her way through this son. I hope you can. It's a terrible thing that's happened to all of us."

"Ooh it is....aye, it is." Before he spoke again Podraic thought about what his father had just said and about what he hadn't told him. "But what about you, dad, how are you coping?"

"I suppose like all the rest of the family, I'm doing the best I can. It's not easy, but what can you do? Our Tommy's gone and there's nothing any of us can do to bring him back. It breaks my heart to think about it and it angers me every time I think how it happened. There's no sense to be made out of it, and to tell you the truth, son, I don't even try and I told your mother the same thing. It's Molly my heart goes out to. As if she hadn't been through enough already. Your mother and I are worried sick about her and wish she'd stayed longer with us in Coleraine. If nothing else, we were able to keep an eye on her, at least for awhile. She's back at her work now, but only working a few days each week. It'll be awhile, I'm sure, before she's strong enough to go back to her work full time."

Podraic sat thoughtfully watching the road as the car passed the show grounds and headed up towards the old cemetery. It was a roundabout way to go home, but probably just as fast as trying to drive through the town so close to Christmas. But perhaps his father had other reasons for taking the longer way home.

"How long are you here for, son?"

"A couple of weeks at the most, and then I'm off to Newry. That's how things stand right now and I have no reason to believe anything different. I will get home again just before I leave for Africa. And who knows? I might even get back for a weekend in between. Newry's not that far and the train service isn't that bad...as long as you're not in a hurry."

His father smiled and nodded approvingly. "Aye...well that would be grand. It's something for all of us to look forward to, especially now. It'll be awhile before we see you again. And you know, son, if it comes to that, sure your mother and I could always drive down to Newry."

"Aye, you could do that too."

"Maybe we will then, it would be good for all of us."

"Dad, what about Bertie and Aggie? Did Bertie get home?"

"He did indeed, he arrived the day before yesterday. I picked him up at the airport and drove him home. It was his first time on an aeroplane, which is more than I can say."

"And Aggie...."

"Oh, I think she's doing alright. She's been spending time with

Molly whenever she gets the chance. I think it's helped both of them. They're a lot alike you know, and I think that helps too. It's hard to believe she'll be finished school this year. I'm not sure she's made up her mind what she wants to do, but whatever it is, she'll do well if she puts her mind to it."

"I don't doubt it for a minute. And Bertie, what about him? Do you think he'll come back?"

"Och, I wouldn't think so. He seems happy enough where he is and he's done well for himself in England, something your mother's been slow to accept, for you know what she's like, God bless her. If she had her way you'd all be living in Ireland and right here in Coleraine."

Podraic smiled. He knew his mother well. "Aye, I suppose we would."

Chapter Twenty-one

Opposite the distillery warehouse Aggie hurriedly turned the corner into Chapel Square, on her way from the centre of the town. In her coat pocket she lightly caressed the small gift she had bought for the young man she loved. It wasn't much, but it was something she wanted him to have. Two weeks earlier they had agreed to meet one last time before Christmas. At the top of Chapel Square she crossed the road and immediately saw him standing in the doorway of the shirt factory. She could easily recognize him by what he was wearing, for he always wore the same tan raincoat, the coat he had spread on the grass when they were together. The shirt factory was closer to her home than she would have liked and it wasn't a very private place either, but it would have to do. There was no time to walk beyond the outskirts of the town as they had done so often the previous summer.

"I can't stay long, honestly I can't," she said, almost out of breath from her brisk walk through the town, "but I wanted so much to see you. I've missed you and what with all that's happened, I wasn't sure I'd see you before Christmas."

"I know..." the young man said softly, nodding his head in agreement, for he too had wondered the same thing. "I've been thinking a lot about you over the past few days, and about us, and about your family and the terrible thing that's happened, and.... and about other things as well." He hesitated, not quite certain if he should tell her all that was going through his mind or keep his thoughts to himself. As soon as he said it, he wished he had not mentioned the other things.

"What is it....?"

"Oh, it's just that...."

"What?"

"It's just that lately, I can't help thinking if what's happened will make it more difficult for us. I don't mean the way you feel about me or the way I feel about you. No...that's not what's bothering me."

"Well, what is it then?"

"It's only that I sometimes wonder how your family will feel about us after what's happened."

"David, what are you saying?"

"Oh it's just a feeling I have that maybe it will be harder for us to see each other, I mean when your parents find out. They don't know about us, or I don't think they do, but sooner or later they're bound to discover we've been seeing each other. We both know Coleraine's not a big place and there's not many secrets about the place either. Both my parents know I'm seeing you and they've known for some time. My father saw us that day last summer on our walk back into the town, and one of the neighbours made a point of telling my mother she'd seen us together. My mother told me as much and she made it clear she was none too pleased when she found out."

"Well I don't think mine do, but who knows? I suppose it's possible someone has said something to them. Not that it matters, for they've not breathed a word of it to me. Besides, what can they say? My father was a protestant when my mother first met him and I think at heart he still is, no matter what others may think. I doubt that he would say anything to me, nor do I think he cares much one way or the other what people might say. No, he's not like that and he brought us up that way too. If anyone says anything to me, it's likely to be my mother, but I'm not even sure she would either."

She moved closer to him, her voice full of resolve. "I won't stop seeing you, no matter what anyone says."

"I know that...."

"It's the truth and I don't want to hear you saying that kind of thing ever again. Promise me....tell me you won't say that again," she said, more determined than ever to put what he had said behind them.

"I won't....I promise."

For what seemed longer than it really was, they stood silently in the shelter of the doorway, each in their own way wondering if it would really be that easy in the days and months ahead to ignore what was happening around them. The young man, in particular, wondered if what had happened to Aggie's family was only a sign of things to come. It seemed all too likely, now that the British Prime Minister had ordered troops into Northern Ireland following the outbreak of violence in Belfast, and in the Catholic Bogside area of Derry. In Belfast, entire streets had been burned to the ground and Catholics driven from their homes. It was something he preferred not to think about and he would try to put it out of his mind. He loved her and that's all that seemed to matter. Somehow the future would take care of itself.

"Here, this is for you, David; open it when you get home," she whispered, pressing her small gift into his hand. "I hope you like it."

"Oh, Aggie, I'm sure I will.

"I love you....you know that, don't you?"

"Of course I do, silly."

"Then say it.... tell me you do."

"I love you."

"Well...?"

"Well what?"

"Show me," she said, her dark eyes flashing in anticipation, as she eased herself closer.

The young man glanced quickly up and down the street and seeing no one, took her in his arms and kissed her, gently at first, and then more passionately. As she moved closer, he could feel her soft body against his and at that moment wished more than anything they were in a more private place.

"Aggie, I love you... and this, this is for you." He reached into his raincoat pocket and withdrew a small unwrapped box. Taking her hand, he gently placed a silver signet ring on her finger.

"Oh, David, what a wonderful gift," she said, tearfully, raising her hand in front of her face to admire the small ring on her finger. "Oh, it is lovely and now, every time I look at it, I will think of you."

"Aggie, I do love you."

"Forever and ever?"

"Yes, forever."

"No matter what happens?"

"No matter what..." he replied earnestly, holding her as long as he dared and releasing her only at the sound of an approaching motor car.

Chapter Twenty-two

Mary sat by the window in the front room watching the street for any sign of her husband and the car that would bring Podraic from the railway station. He wasn't expected much before one o'clock and then, only if the train was running on time. The Derry train was frequently late these days and it was anybody's guess if it would arrive on time. She knew that well enough, but had made up her mind, after tidying up the house for the second time that morning, to go into the room anyway just in case he arrived on time after all. She was determined to be at the front door to greet him when he stepped out of the car. On the news there had been more violence reported in Belfast and she wondered when it would all end. They were fortunate indeed, to live in a town like Coleraine, she thought, a town where things remained relatively peaceful in spite of what seemed to be happening in other parts of the country. It saddened her to think how cruel people could be to other human beings and she wondered how long it would take before they realized there had to be a better way to settle their grievances.

A few days ago two men had landed on the moon again, and

they had brought them safely home to earth in time for Christmas. She thought it strange that mankind could achieve something that wonderful and yet no one seemed able to bring people together to live in peace.

A short time earlier she had been crying and had gone upstairs to wash and dry her face before returning to her seat by the window. It happened often these days, sometimes without warning, and mostly when she was alone as she was this afternoon. Sitting alone was something she needed to do now more than ever, for it gave her a chance to gather up her thoughts and decide how best they might celebrate Christmas given all that had happened. It wouldn't be easy for any of them, but she couldn't bear the thought of not celebrating Christmas as they had always done. That would be even worse. Christmas had always been such an important part of their lives and she was determined that this year would be no exception. She had moved Tommy's picture and set it on the table close to where they would open the presents on Christmas day. That too, was the right thing to do. They would all do the best they could, no matter how painful it might be. Bertie had spent a good part of the morning with her and in his own way had managed to cheer her up by reminding her of the many things in her life that were good. At one point she had almost laughed with him over something he said about his father. And having dear Podraic home, even for a brief visit, would help them all. He would be able to comfort Molly in a way that would help her deal with the terrible thing that had happened in her young life. She was quite sure of it, and in her heart just as certain he would be able to do the same for her.

She reached up and touched the small silver cross hanging about her neck, the one her husband had given her soon after they were married. It will be alright, she thought. With God's help we'll get through this. Having all the family together for Christmas was what she wanted most, especially now.

Tomorrow was Christmas Eve and Molly too would be home to spend Christmas with her family.

Railway Road
Tuesday 12 June 1973

Chapter Twenty-three

Mary started up the street towards the dry cleaners and for no reason at all changed her mind and walked back to the Pork Shop she had passed just a few minutes earlier. The shop was busy for a Tuesday afternoon. Inside, the owner was waiting on a handful of customers. "Hello, Mrs Thompson," he shouted, expertly wrapping a pound of sausages in pink butchers' paper and tying it tightly from a bundle of light string. "There..." he said, passing the package over the glass counter top to the woman standing in front of him. "Is there anything else, Mrs. McCurdy?" The woman shook her head and handed him the exact change. Mary waited her turn and then ordered a pound of minced pork.

"That's turned into a nice day after all, Mrs. Thompson."

"Indeed it has, Mr Armstrong," she said, nodding her head in agreement.

He scooped up a handful of minced pork from a large mound of mince on a metal tray, and placed it on the white scales at the end of the counter. The red pointer swung across the face of the scale and settled just a hair beyond the one pound mark. "I'd say that's close enough," he said, smiling with obvious satisfaction. With a single motion of his hand he knotted the string and passed the parcel over the counter.

"Will there be anything else, missus?"

"No, sure I think that'll do...."

She was still debating whether to bring home a few slices of vegetable roll as she handed him a five pound note and waited for her change. It would do very nicely for supper tomorrow night, especially with new potatoes and fresh peas and it would save another trip into the town, she thought, as she slipped the minced pork into her shopping bag. He saw her hesitate for a moment. It happened often, mostly with women, and he knew from years of experience that a customer's uncertainty frequently resulted in an additional purchase of something that was not on the shopping list when they walked into the shop.

"Are you sure?"

"Well on second thought, maybe you had better wrap up half a pound of the sliced vegetable roll while you're at it." She was quite certain now as she handed back the change he had just placed on the counter.

"That's the lot, then, Mrs Thompson," he said with a broad smile.

"Aye...that'll do nicely, thank you Mr Armstrong."

As she turned to leave she glanced quickly at the clock on the wall. It was almost twenty five minutes to three. She had spent more time on the street than she had intended and she still had a few more messages to run. It was just as well she had told her husband she would walk home on her own when she was finished.

Outside on the street a young woman, walking in the other direction, waved to her as they passed on opposite sides of the street. It was one of Aggie's school friends from Loretta Convent. For the life of her, she couldn't remember the wee girl's name, and it annoyed her that she couldn't put a name to the face. And what made it worse was the fact that she had seen her in chapel only a week earlier. Mary waved back and continued up Railway Road to the Coleraine & Portrush Laundry. At the top of the street she suddenly remembered she'd forgotten to ask her husband for the dry cleaning slip. Or was it the other way around and he just hadn't bothered to give it to her. That was more likely, she thought, as she passed Hart's dairy and rounded the corner. No matter, for she knew Mrs Connolly would find it just the same. If there was nobody else in the shop she'd likely be there for awhile, a good five minutes and maybe longer. Mrs Connolly was a great talker and not a bit shy in voicing her opinion on almost any subject. Or giving the odd customer a piece of her mind, if she thought it was warranted. Rarely did anyone take offence and if they did she paid them no heed for to her way of thinking, if they didn't like what she had to say they could always take their laundry somewhere else. But she enjoyed a good laugh all the same and for the most part was popular with her customers regardless of who they were.

Mary opened the door and walked in.

The shop was empty.

"Hello, Mrs Connolly."

The woman behind the counter smiled and set down her tea cup. "How many pieces did you have Mrs Thompson?"

"Just two, a blazer and a pair of trousers, but I'm out without the receipt."

"Oh, never mind, I'll find them easy enough."

"That's very good of you Mrs Connolly."

"Och sure it's no bother...no bother at all, and anyway there's not much back there this afternoon so it shouldn't take long to find them.... it'll only take me a minute, you'll see," she said, cheerfully, disappearing at once into the back of the shop. A short time later she reappeared with two plastic bags over her arm. "There you are Mrs Thompson, that's the lot, then, one blazer and one pair of trousers. Here, let me put them on one hanger; it'll be easier carried that way." Mary paid for the dry cleaning and put the change in her purse. She thanked Mrs Connolly and turned quickly toward the door, but not soon enough. "Did you hear what happened to Nelly Bell's son, the one who worked on the buses? I swear I never heard the like of it and him a great church man and all."

♣

Thompson washed his hands at the kitchen sink. He'd been out in the garden for a short time and was pleased with the way things were coming along. It was a small garden. He had kept it that way by design. Just big enough to manage, it provided the family with some of the fresh vegetables they needed over the summer months, things like lettuce and cabbage that always tasted so much better when they were picked fresh from the garden. This year he had also planted a small row of parsley and a row of parsnips and carrots. The small greenhouse attached to the back of the house provided more than enough tomatoes to last them all summer long and what they didn't need they shared with their neighbours. Puttering about in the backyard when the weather was pleasant was something he had come to enjoy now that he had a bit more time on his hands. Caring for the larger garden required a little more effort on his part. The rhubarb, on the other hand, seemed to manage quite well on its own and required no attention whatsoever other than cutting the stalks as they ripened. Left on its own, it grew contentedly in a sunny corner of the garden. The weeds, he noticed, were getting ahead of him again, not an uncommon situation he had to admit, but he decided to leave them and to tackle the job another day when he had more time. And besides, it was too nice a day to be bent over a patch of ground pulling out stubborn weeds. At least he'd made a good start on what needed to be done. The rest he could always finish tomorrow or the day after if the weather held. June had turned out to be a lovely month and there was no reason to believe the warm weather they were experiencing would not continue for at least another week or so.

He glanced at his watch. It was early yet, but he decided to go ahead and set the table anyway. It would give him something to do and help take his mind off other things. Later, he would put on the kettle and make them both a nice cup of tea. Mary should be home by then and she'd have plenty of time to put her feet up and enjoy a cup before she started supper. Since he had grown older, he was content to help around the house. That was not always the case for there was a time when it wouldn't have occurred to him to lift a cup let alone set the table or cook a meal. Mary didn't seem to mind either, so long as he stayed out of her way. When the children were small he seldom made a meal other than on those rare occasions when their mother travelled to Galway to spend a few days with her parents. He wasn't much of a cook and he couldn't remember the youngsters ever expressing regret that they weren't left with their father more often.

He hadn't said anything to Mary, although he had intended to mention it earlier in the day, but lately he'd been thinking it might be nice to take a run over to Rathlin Island before the summer ended. He had not ever been there and it was something he had always wanted to do. They had talked about going a few years earlier, but after all that had happened it didn't seem to be the right thing to do. Their hearts just weren't in it. Already he had made several inquiries and learned that the boat left from Ballycastle harbour in the morning and returned in the late afternoon just in time for a fish and chip supper before they started back for Coleraine. He'd found out too there was a public house at Church Bay, close to where the boat came in, where they could order a large pot of tea and have their sandwiches in the pub or outside on the lawn before setting out to explore the island. He might even have a pint.

Molly would come too, of course, just as they'd always planned. It would do her the world of good to have a bit of an outing. For a young woman she'd had more than her share of trouble and he wondered aloud how it was that some people manage to go through life with little or no bother at all. Life hardly scratches them while others are so badly knocked about it's all they can do just to keep on going. It didn't seem right somehow, especially when you think of the rascals running about the countryside that never seemed to have a day's trouble in their whole life. At both ends of the table he set out a knife and fork and a teaspoon, taking care to make sure each piece was arranged neatly at right angles to the edge of the table. Poor Molly didn't deserve any of it, he told himself, as he picked up two large dinner plates and set them down at opposite ends of the table.

When it happened, he recalled painfully, they had both wanted Molly to come home to Coleraine. It seemed the right thing to do and with her qualifications she would have had no trouble finding a suitable nursing position at the hospital. But she was determined to stay where she was. Even Podraic couldn't persuade her to reconsider. It was what she wanted and she would hear of nothing else. And when little Tommy died it came as no surprise that he would be buried in Ballycastle. Her decision to remain there didn't sit well with her mother and, if he was honest with himself, he wasn't happy with it either. Mary believed it would be better for all of them if Molly was closer to home. She was probably right, but he knew in his heart it was Molly's decision to make.

For months Molly blamed herself for not leaving her friend's home earlier that evening and putting little Tommy to bed at his usual time. She wondered too why she had left the house in the first place when the weather that night was so bad. It wasn't that she had to go, she said, it was just that she thought it would be nice to have a night out. She had shared her feelings of guilt with both of them and together they had worked their way through it as best they could.

He remembered too, that at the beginning she refused to talk about putting a headstone on the grave which only added to her mother's distress. It was too soon. She needed more time, she told them, to come to grips with what had happened. But in the months that followed he managed to persuade her it was something she needed to do. He told her that without some kind of a marker it was difficult to move on. In the end she bravely accepted her father's advice.

He stood by the kitchen window reflecting on all that had happened since the bombing in Ballycastle. Things were worse now than he ever could have imagined. Over the past few years sectarian violence in the six counties had reached staggering proportions. Last year alone, he recalled, nearly five hundred people were murdered at the hands of the Provisional Irish Republican Army and Loyalist paramilitary groups. The events of Bloody Sunday were still fresh in his mind. In Derry, the British Army opened fire on marchers who were protesting the introduction of the Internment law which allowed the army and the police to arrest and detain individuals without trial. Fourteen people were killed that Sunday afternoon when rioting broke out at the end of the march. And in July of that same year, after a failed attempt to negotiate with the British Government for the return of Northern Ireland to the Irish Republic, the IRA retaliated by detonating twenty two bombs in less than an hour in the city of Belfast. No warning was given. Nine people were killed and a hundred and thirty were injured. It became known as Bloody Friday. And more recently, he had heard disturbing new reports of the torture and assassination of nationalists just because they were Catholics. In Belfast, Protestant and Catholic families who had lived peacefully in the same community for years, were forced to leave their homes and ordered to live with their own kind. "God help us," he said wearily, shaking his head in disbelief. "Who would have thought it would come to this?"

He placed the last of the supper dishes on the kitchen table and turned back towards the pantry. As he did so, he heard a loud explosion that shook the house.

At that precise moment, the blue Ford Cortina tore itself apart from the force of an exploding two hundred pound bomb. The blast tore out the front of two shops and set them on fire. Flying glass and pieces of metal and debris from other buildings caught people on the street below as they ran for cover to escape the force of the explosion. A huge cloud of dense black smoke poured from the spot where the car had been and rose slowly into the still afternoon air.

"What in the name of God is that?" he shouted in shocked disbelief. At first he wasn't sure what to make of it. For an instant he thought it might have come from the direction of Maxwell's quarry on the outskirts of the town. It was common enough to hear the sound of an explosion when they were blasting rock with dynamite. But he couldn't remember ever hearing an explosion that loud coming from the quarry. It was too powerful. Then it occurred to him that maybe there had been a terrible accident at the gasworks. A large explosion in the gasworks would be powerful enough to shake houses on this side of the river. But that didn't make sense either when he thought about it for as near as he could tell it hadn't come from that direction. It sounded more as if it had come from the bottom of the Lodge Road or perhaps from somewhere near the centre of the town, but he couldn't be certain of that either without going outside to see for himself. At that moment, he wasn't so sure that was something he really wanted to do. God knows what he might find.

It was then he remembered Mary was somewhere in the town, either on the way home or worse, finishing the last of her shopping. "Ooh....oh my God," he cried, rushing into the street, leaving the porch door wide open behind him.

By now a handful of people had emerged from their homes and stood quietly in the middle of the road exchanging nervous glances and looking in the general direction of the town. Panic stricken he turned and ran quickly to where the car was parked on the opposite side of the street. Just as he reached it, he suddenly realized the keys were in his jacket pocket and in his present state of mind he hadn't the faintest notion where he had thrown it. He hesitated for a moment, then turned back and started running down the street. As he neared the bottom of the street he heard the clanging of an emergency vehicle from somewhere close by and then another from the direction of Long Commons. On Adelaide Avenue a fire engine raced passed him, turned the corner without stopping, and accelerated rapidly down the Lodge Road towards a pillar of smoke that was rising over the town. Rounding the corner he could see it plainly now, black and sinister, swirling upwards behind the row of large terrace houses on the Lodge Road. Not far from where he stopped briefly to catch his breath, three uniformed police officers bolted down the steps of the RUC barracks and ran the short distance to Railway Road.

At the foot of the Lodge Road Thompson hurriedly turned the corner into Railway Road and unwittingly stumbled into the middle of the street. He stopped abruptly, almost falling over a large pile of smoking rubble lying on the street directly in front of him.

"God almighty....what have they done?"

In all his fifty one years he had never witnessed anything like this. It was as if he were standing in the middle of a war zone, the kind of thing he'd seen only on newsreels during the Second World War. He stood motionless, clenching his hands tightly against his sides as he struggled to come to grips with the carnage that lay around him. The scene on the street was almost too much to comprehend and instinctively he closed his eyes, and for a moment wanted to turn and walk away from it all, but that was something he knew he could not do.

Pulling himself together he slowly became aware of other people on the street. Some were running from the scene screaming. Others, with blood flowing from open wounds in their head and face, wandered aimlessly about the street crying out for help. Some were unable to move at all and just lay where they had fallen. He turned to look away and as he did so he saw bodies on the street not far from where he stood. Then he saw a woman with blood streaming down her face holding a small child in her arms. He reached down to help an elderly woman trying to get on her feet, and as he put his arm around her he suddenly remembered again why he had rushed out of the house just minutes earlier.

"Ooh... Mary....Oh my poor darling, where in God's name are you?" He wandered back and forth searching the street and doing what he could to help the people around him, all the while dreading that at any moment he would see her lying somewhere on the road. Then it dawned on him that he couldn't remember what she was wearing when he dropped her off on the Lodge Road less than an hour ago. Oh dear God... how was he to find her if he couldn't even remember what she was wearing? What kind of a man was he anyway that he couldn't remember what his own wife was wearing just a short time ago? In his confusion all he could recall was the colour of the shopping bag swaying by her side as she turned the corner and cheerfully waved back at him. He thought she might have been wearing a pair of dark blue or black shoes, but he couldn't even be sure of that. What he did remember soberly was what she had told him before she got out of the car. She said she would drop into the Pork Shop on the way home. Ooh God, no....not there, but that's exactly what she had said. In desperation, he crossed the street again and frantically searched the pavement and the road near the front of the shop, but she was nowhere to be seen. The shop itself was empty. A short distance from where he stood on the street, not far from where the car bomb exploded, a young nurse and an ambulance driver were covering someone on a stretcher with a white sheet. It was no one he knew. As he watched, private cars began arriving to help transport the injured to hospital. There were so many in need of help and at that moment it occurred to him that maybe he should have brought the car after all. Had he done so he might have been able to do more.

He turned away and walked back to the other side of the road and for a short time stood in the doorway of the Constitution office trying to sort out what he should do next. God knows he had to find her, but he had looked everywhere and he didn't know where else to look. He wished now he had parked the car and gone with her when the thought crossed his mind earlier in the afternoon. There was nothing he had to do at home that couldn't have waited. The garden could be weeded anytime and even if he missed a week what difference would it really make? That's what he should have done and he reproached himself bitterly for not doing it. Perhaps if he had, she would be safely home by now. At the very least he would have known where she was. A wave of panic swept over him at the realization she could be lying almost anywhere, hidden beneath the debris that had fallen on the street and he wouldn't even be aware of it. "Oh Mary darling, where are you?"

Shaken, he wandered aimlessly across the street and for several agonizing moments stood in the middle of the road confused and fearful now that he might not find her alive. He staggered, almost falling over a large piece of twisted metal he had not seen in his haste to double back to the other side of the street. He would start all over again for he had to find her. What else could he do? He had to keep looking.

Then, as he turned to look in the direction of the railway station, he thought he saw her in the distance, or a woman who looked like her, sitting on the stone wall opposite Christie's picture house. From where he stood, he couldn't be certain it was her. He still didn't remember what she was wearing and again it angered him that he had not paid more attention when she stepped out of the car. But as he started to run towards her he saw the shopping bag lying at her feet and he knew instantly it was Mary.

"Ooh....it is her....thank God she's safe."

"Willie, over here."

"Ooh, my poor darling I see you."

"Willie, I'm so frightened."

"Aye... and no wonder. I've been looking everywhere for you. And God help me, I was beginning to think I would never find you. I searched the whole street, but I couldn't find you....I couldn't find you anywhere. Oh dear God, I couldn't find you. And just now I thought I'd lost you...."

He threw his arms around her and wept.

Together they sat on the stone wall and held each other as if their lives depended upon it. Mary buried her head in his shoulder and quietly sobbed, oblivious to what was happening on the street around her.

"Willie....I am so afraid....and to think if I hadn't stopped to talk to Mrs Henry on the street or for that matter changed my mind for no reason at all and decided to go to the Pork Shop first. I might have been....."

"Ooh, my poor darling."

"I don't know why I did it...."

"God only knows...but I thank God you did."

"Willie....take me home. Ooh dear God, please take me home," she whispered, her voice still trembling.

He took her hand and gently helped her to her feet. "Aye, love, but not that way. It's enough that one of us had to see it."

A short time later, the second car bomb exploded in Hanover Place, sending shoppers scurrying from the streets to the safety of their own homes, terrified that bombs had been planted in other parts of the town. And for a second time, on that bright summer afternoon, a sinister cloud of dark tortured smoke rose above the town and drifted slowly over the Bann. Above the ancient town a gull rode the wind and the river flowed unheeded to the sea.

------- O -------

The novel is dedicated to the memory of
the individuals who lost their lives in the
bombing of Coleraine on June 12, 1973

†